PENGUIN BOOKS

THE DARK

John McGahern was born in Dublin in 1934 and brought
up in the west of Ireland. He is a graduate of University
College, Dublin. He is the author of three collections of
short stories and six novels, *The Barracks* (1963), *The
Dark* (1965), *The Leavetaking* (1974), *The Pornographer*
(1979), *Amongst Women* (1990), which was shortlisted for
the Booker Prize, and most recently, *That They May Face
the Rising Sun*. John McGahern lives in Co. Leitrim.

JOHN McGAHERN

The Dark

PENGUIN BOOKS

PENGUIN BOOKS
Published by the Penguin Group
Penguin Group (USA) Inc., 375 Hudson Street, New York, New York 10014, U.S.A.
Penguin Books Ltd, 80 Strand, London WC2R 0RL, England
Penguin Books Australia Ltd, 250 Camberwell Road, Camberwell, Victoria 3124, Australia
Penguin Books Canada Ltd, 10 Alcorn Avenue, Toronto, Ontario, Canada M4V 3B2
Penguin Books India (P) Ltd, 11 Community Centre, Panchsheel Park, New Delhi – 110 017, India
Penguin Books (N.Z.) Ltd, Cnr Rosedale and Airborne Roads, Albany, Auckland, New Zealand
Penguin Books (South Africa) (Pty) Ltd, 24 Sturdee Avenue,
Rosebank, Johannesburg 2196, South Africa

Penguin Books Ltd, Registered Offices: 80 Strand, London WC2R 0RL, England

First published in Great Britain by Faber and Faber Limited 1965
First published in the United States of America by Alfred A. Knopf, Inc. 1966
Published in Penguin Books 1983
This edition published in Penguin Books 2002

3   5   7   9   10   8   6   4   2

Copyright © John McGahern, 1965
All rights reserved

PUBLISHER'S NOTE
This is a work of fiction. Names, characters, places, and incidents either
are the product of the author's imagination or are used ficticiously, and any
resemblance to actual persons, living or dead, business establishments,
events, or locales is entirely coincidental.

LIBRARY OF CONGRESS CATALOGING IN PUBLICATION DATA
McGahern, John, 1934–
The dark / John McGahern.
p.   cm.
ISBN 0 14 02.7795 1 (pbk. : alk. paper)
1. Fathers and sons—Fiction.   2. Ireland—Fiction.   I. Title.
PR6063.A2176 D3 2002
823'.914—dc21   20011054859

Printed in the United States of America
Set in Plantin

Except in the United States of America, this book is sold
subject to the condition that it shall not, by way of trade or otherwise,
be lent, re-sold, hired out, or otherwise circulated without the publisher's
prior consent in any form of binding or cover other than that in which
it is published and without a similar condition including this
condition being imposed on the subsequent purchaser.

to ANNIKKI LAAKSI

1

"Say what you said because i know."

"I didn't say anything."

"Out with it I tell you."

"I don't know I said anything."

"F-U-C-K is what you said, isn't it? That profane and ugly word. Now do you think you can bluff your way out of it?"

"I didn't mean, it just came out."

"The filth that's in your head came out, you mean. And I'm going to teach you a lesson for once. You'd think there'd be some respect for your dead mother left in the house. And trying to sing dumb—as if butter wouldn't melt. But I'll teach you."

He took the heavy leather strap he used for sharpening his razor from its nail on the side of the press.

"Come on with me. Upstairs. I'll teach you a lesson for once. I'll teach you a lesson for once," he said with horrible measured passion through his teeth, the blood mounted to his face. "I'll teach you a lesson this house won't forget in a hurry."

"I didn't mean it, Daddy. I didn't mean it, it just slipped out."

"Up the stairs. March. I'm telling you. Up the stairs."

By the shoulder Mahoney pushed him out the door into the hallway towards the stairs.

"March, march, march," he kept grinding as they went. "Quickly. No, not in there," when he turned for the room where they both slept together. "Into the girls' room. This'll have to be witnessed. I'll teach a lesson this house won't forget."

The two large beds where all the girls slept faced the door, the little table between them, and above it on the wall the picture of the Ascension. A plywood wardrobe and a black leather armchair stood beside the empty fireplace. Mona rose out of the bedclothes in fright at their coming.

"I'm going to teach this gent a lesson. Your sister can be witness of this. Now off with your clothes. I'm going to teach you a lesson. Quick. Strip. Off with your clothes."

Slowly, in a dazed horror, he got off his jacket and wept.

"No. I didn't mean it, Daddy. It just slipped out."

"Off with your jersey. Quick. We can't stand here all day," a white froth showed on his lips. The eyes stared out beyond the walls of the room. The belt twitched against his trousers, an animal's tail.

"Off with the trousers. Off with trousers."

"No, no."

"Off with the trousers, I said."

He just moved closer. He didn't lift a hand, as if the stripping compelled by his will alone gave him pleasure.

"Off with the trousers," and with frightened weeping the trousers were let slip down around the ankles on the floor.

"Off with the shirt," he ground quietly, and when the shirt was off the boy stood completely naked. With the belt he pointed to the armchair.

"Into that chair with you. On your mouth and nose. I'll give your arse something it won't forget in a hurry."

"No, Daddy, no. I didn't mean," he gave one last whimper but he had to lie in the chair, lie there and wait as a broken animal. Something in him snapped. He couldn't control his water and it flowed from him over the leather of the seat. He'd never imagined horror such as this, waiting naked for the leather to come down on his flesh, would it ever come, it was impossible and yet nothing could be much worse than this waiting.

"I'll teach you a lesson for once," and then he cried out as the leather came, exploding with a shot on the leather of the armrest over his ear, his whole body stiff, sweat breaking, and it was impossible to realize he hadn't actually been hit yet.

"No, no, no," he cried as he tried to rise.

"Don't move. Don't move. Move and I'll cut that arse off you. I'm only giving you a taste of what you're going to get. I'm just showing you and shut that shouting," and he was willed by fear back on his mouth and nose, not able to move, shivering fits beginning to come, and the anguish and squalor was impossible, but would the black leather cut across his flesh this time, it was horrible and worse than death to think.

It came as it came before, a rifle crack on the armrest, the same hysterical struggle, and he hadn't been hit yet, it was unreal.

"Don't move and shut that shouting," and when he was reasonably still except for the shivering and weeping, the leather came for the third time exactly as before. He didn't know anything or what he was doing or where the room was

9

when the leather exploded on the black armrest beside where his ear was.

"Shut up that racket and get on your feet. Quick. And shut up. It's on the bare skin you'll get it the next time but that taste'll do for this time. Get your clothes on you. You can count yourself lucky. Get up. Get up."

It was such a struggle to realize it was over. He had to try to get on his feet out of the chair, it was a kind of tearing, and to stand naked on the floor. The shivering fits of crying came and went, but quieter. He was only aware of Mona's frightened wailing in the bed when Mahoney shouted, "You in the bed shut up before you get cause. Shut up now. Let that be a lesson to you. I don't know whether it's sick you are or foxing in that bed these last days. And you—you get your clothes, and waste no time getting downstairs," he turned to the naked boy before he left the room, his face still red and heated, the leather hanging dead in his hand.

It was a real struggle to get each piece of clothing on after he'd gone, the hands clumsy and shaking. The worst was the vapoury rush of thoughts, he couldn't get any grip on what had happened to him, he'd never known such a pit of horror as he'd touched, nothing seemed to matter any more. His mother had gone away years before and left him to this. Day of sunshine he'd picked wild strawberries for her on the railway she was dying.

"Did he hit you at all?" Mona was asking from the bed.

"No."

The word opened such a floodgate that he had to hurry out of the room with the last of his clothes in his hands, by the front door out to the old bolted refuge of the lavatory, with the breeze blowing in its one airhole. There they all rushed hours as these to sit in the comforting darkness and reek of Jeyes Fluid to weep and grope their way in hatred and self-pity back to some sort of calm.

2

THEY ALL GOT BEATINGS, OFTEN FOR NO REASON, BECAUSE THEY laughed when he was in foul humour, but they learned to make him suffer—to close their life against him and to leave him to himself.

"I'm told nothing in this house, never. I might as well be a leper but who's bringing you up alone without help, who's earning the bread," he'd complain.

They'd listen silently, with grave faces: but once they'd turn to each other they'd smile cruelly. He couldn't have it both ways. He'd put himself outside and outside they'd make him stay. Neither brutality nor complaining could force a way in but it was not so easy to keep him out when he changed and offered them an outing, to Duffy's circus, or a day on the river.

"It'd be nice to make a day of it fishing tomorrow."

They'd make no answer, they'd watch him and each other, they didn't trust.

"Why can't you speak out? We could go after first Mass and bring sandwiches and make a day of it."

"It'd be nice," they weren't sure, they didn't trust enough to want to go.

"We'd be able to get bottles of lemonade to drink with the sandwiches at Knockvicar. We might get a few pike too."

And suddenly they trusted again because they wanted, he was their father, this time might be different and happy. They laughed. Tomorrow they'd go together in the tarred boat to Knockvicar.

The old boat held together by tar and pitch and sand was moored under a sally on the river, dead leaves of the sally on the ribs and floorboards with the fish scales.

They took their places in the boat before he untied it, and with one knee on the edge drove it out into the stream, and clambered on to the rowing-seat while it was moving. They began to let out the spoons as he pulled.

"Watch now. Hold the lines tight. I hear a twenty-pounder coming round by Moran's Bay on a motor-bike," he joked and they laughed but their fingers trembled on the white lines, feeling the vibration of the spoons and then someone shouted.

"I have a one, Daddy. He's pulling. Quick."

"Watch that you don't give him slack line. Hold him," he shouted back. He started to row fiercely, shouting, "Try and keep the boat shifting," as he let go the oars to take the line. They took his place at the oars but they were too excited to pull much.

"Try and keep the boat on the move," he had to say.

They watched him drag the fighting fish close, hand over hand.

"He's a good one. He's trying for the bottom."

12

And then the fish was sliding towards the boat on the surface, the mouth open, showing the vicious teeth and the whiteness and the spoon hooked in the roof of the mouth. He would make his last fight at the side of the boat, it was dangerous if the hooks weren't in firmly, he could shake them free, the sinking of the heart as they rattled loose. But Mahoney had leaned out and got him by the gills with his fingers. He was lifting him into the boat.

"He's four pounds. That's a start, I'm telling you."

They watched the pike on the floorboards and they gloated, the gleaming yellow stripes across the back and the white swollen belly, the jaws with the vicious rows of teeth snapping air as blood trickled from the gills.

When the boat was moving again, all the spoons rescued from the bottom and spinning, the bell for second Mass came clear over the water.

"It's only eleven yet and we have a right pike," he said as he rowed. Soon the noise of cars and speech crossing the bridge in the distance on the way to Mass mingled with the constant rippling of the oars. The last bell rang when there was quiet.

"They're starting into Mass now. If you're not early afoot and at first Mass there's no length left in the day. It's gone and wasted."

"And we've a pike caught, Daddy."

"We have and most of the day left and on the river."

"I've a one this time," a shout rose. Another fish was hooked. The same struggle started. And the boat was sliding in its own ripple in the narrow reaches of the river, in the calm under the leaning trees of Oakport, wood strawberries in the moss under the heaviest beeches, cattle in the fields the side facing the wood. He rowed that way under the trees to Knockvicar, where he bought lemonade in the post office, and they ate the sandwiches on the river bank. Afterwards he slept with his straw hat over his face while they left the bottles back and played.

He woke in less than the hour, but he was drowsy and different; though he said, "This is the way to live," as he pushed the boat with an oar out from the bank, the effort to still praise the day was growing strained, and a wary silence grew over the boat turned towards home. Mahoney rowed in silence, it was easy in the calm of Oakport, but once they left the narrower reaches he had to fight the wind.

"A sleep in the middle of the day if you're not used to it gives you a damned headache," he was tiring, cursing every time the waves fouled his stroke, and in this rough water they let the lines cross and tangle without noticing, they were so intent and anxious. When they did it was too late and once he saw the mess his growing frustration turned their way.

"Now do you see," he left the oars. "Too cursed lazy to watch the lines while I break my back against this wind."

Except for one line out on a bamboo rod the spinning spoons had turned the lines into a tangle that'd take hours to loose.

"It'll take a day to get that mess out and to think I brought you out fishing. We have to row home with one bait out. What tempted me to bring you at all. God, O God, such a misfortunate crowd of ignoramuses to be saddled with," he shouted, while they listened in hatred, they shouldn't have trusted, they hadn't even wanted to come out, they could take his throat, but they were afraid to even stir on the seats.

He was grinding his teeth, a habit when he was in a rage, and then he caught two of them and shook them violently.

"Too useless to do anything while I kill myself," he mouthed and only for the dangerous rocking of the boat his rage would have carried him on its own impetus.

"Such a cross to have to live under," he complained back at the oars, and started to pull furiously, the boat lifting against the rock of water, the line on the bamboo rod taut with the speed and the spoon pulled to the surface far behind and glittering.

They sat in silence, the boredom of watching the oars, violence was preferable to this constant nagging. "God, O God, O God, such a curse," at the oars.

The seagulls were screaming over their island of bare rocks ringed with reeds on McCabe's shore as the nag-nag-nag went like a hacksaw across the steel of their hatred.

They carried the fish home in the same dogged silence, with the tangled lines, and there he changed again.

"It was a good day's outing we had anyhow," he enthused.

"It was good," they were utterly watchful.

"We must go on the river oftener."

"It'd be nice to go."

"What about a game of cards?" he took the pack from the window.

"We have to tidy up and get the dinner ready for to-morrow."

"But that won't take you all night. You can manage it later."

"We better scale and gut the pike too, they go bad quick this time. It won't take too long. Then we can play," they evaded.

They gathered in the scullery to do the very little they had to do: scrape the scales of the pike with the big bread-knife, cabbage put with a portion of bacon in the aluminium sauce-pan and the potatoes washed and left ready, the dusk broken by a candle burning on a canister lid in the window.

"Does anyone want a game of cards?" a softly mimicking voice caused a stifled burst of laughing as they finished.

They stood stiff to listen in the scullery. His chair creaked. The habitual hissing he made with his lips when he played alone came. Buttons of his sleeve scraped on the wooden edge.

His hands brushed the soft green surface on the table as he gathered in the cards for the flick-flick of the patient dealing again. A grim smile of understanding showing on the faces in the scullery with the candle flame burning before the shaving-mirror in the window.

"Let him play alone."

3

THE WORST WAS TO HAVE TO SLEEP WITH HIM THE NIGHTS HE
wanted love, strain of waiting for him to come to bed, no hope
of sleep in the waiting—counting and losing the count of the
thirty-two boards across the ceiling, trying to pick out the
darker circles of the knots beneath the varnish. Watch the
moon on the broken brass bells at the foot of the bed. Turn
and listen and turn. Go over the day that was gone, what was
done or left undone, or dream of the dead days with her in
June.

The dreams and passing of time would break with the
noise of the hall door opening, feet on the cement, his habitual
noises as he drank barley water over the dying fire, and at
last the stockinged feet on the stairs.

He was coming and there was nothing to do but wait and
grow hard as stone and lie.

"Are you sleeping?"

The one thing was to keep the eyes shut no matter what and to lie stiff as a board.

"You're asleep so?"

It was such breathing relief to hear the soft plump of his clothes being let fall on the floor. And then the winding of the clock.

A sudden pause instead of him pulling back the sheets, he was fumbling through the heap of clothes on the floor. A match struck and flared in the dark. It was brought close. He could feel the heat on his face. His lids lit up like blood-soaked curtains. With a cry he turned sideways and brought his hands to his face. When he could look the flame had burned down the black char of matchwood to Mahoney's fingers, and his face was ugly with suspicion.

"You were quick to wake?"

He'd have to pull himself together to answer.

"I was sleeping. I felt something."

The match flame had burned out.

"You didn't seem to be sleeping much to me?"

"I was sleeping. I got frightened."

Hatred took the place of fear, and it brought the mastery of not caring much more. No one had right to bring a match burning close to his face in the night to see if he was sleeping or not.

"I was sleeping and you frightened me with the match. Did you want me for anything that you cracked the match?"

"No. I just wanted to see if you were asleep and alright. I didn't mean to frighten you."

At the window he wound the green clock, the key twisted in the silence, he pulled back the clothes, and awkwardly got into bed. The feet were cold as clay as they touched on the way down.

"Will you be able to sleep now?"

"Soon. I'll be able to go to sleep."

"I'm sorry I woke you up. I just cracked the match to see if you were alright. You don't mind now, do you?"

"No. I don't mind. It's alright."

"We're too cooped up in ourselves here. That's the trouble. We haven't had a word for ages together. People need an outing now and again. You'd like a day out, wouldn't you? We could go to town together. We could have tea in the Royal Hotel. It'd be a change. It'd take us out of ourselves. People get cooped up in themselves. You'd like to go to town, wouldn't you?" the voice was growing restless with excitement.

"It'd be nice," the wary answer came, there had been too many of those midnight heart-easings that could go on far into the mornings. All this talk and struggle to get to terms or understanding that'd last for no longer than the sleep of this night. It was always changed by the morning: shame and embarrassment and loathing, the dirty rags of intimacy. The struggle was not his struggle nor the words, and there were worse things in these nights than words.

"In every house there are differences. Things don't all the time run smooth. Though that's not what counts, sure it's not."

"No."

"As long as we know that. That's all that matters. Even though things don't run right. As long as people know that, what happens doesn't matter as long as the feeling between them is right. Then things can't run wrong for long, isn't that right?"

"That's right."

"Even Up Above there was trouble. There's differences everywhere. But that's not what matters. Everyone loses their temper and says things and does things but as long as you know there's love there it doesn't matter. Don't you know I love you no matter what happens?"

19

"I do."

"And you love your father?"

"I do."

"You'll give your father a kiss so?"

The old horror as hands were put about him and the other face closed on his, the sharp stubble grown since the morning and the nose and the kiss, the thread of the half-dried mucus coming away from the other lips in the kiss.

"You don't have to worry about anything. There's no need to be afraid or cry. Your father loves you," and hands drew him closer. They began to move in caress on the back, shoving up the nightshirt, downwards lightly to the thighs and heavily up again, the voice echoing rhythmically the movement of the hands.

"You don't have to worry about anything. Your father loves you. You like that—it's good for you—it relaxes you—it lets you sleep. Would you like me to rub you here? It'll ease wind. You like that? It'll let you sleep."

The words drummed softly as the stroking hands moved on his belly, down and up, touched with the fingers the thighs again, and came again on the back.

"We'll go to town one of these days. We can walk together round the shops and look for a new suit for you in Curleys. We can go to the Royal Hotel for tea."

The hands moved more tensely. The breathing quickened.

"You like that. It's good for you," the voice breathed jerkily now to the stroking hands.

"I like that."

There was nothing else to say, it was better not to think or care, and the hands—the rhythmic words—were a kind of pleasure if thought and loathing could be shut out. The growing hotness and the sweat were the worst but it was better to lie in the arms and not listen except to the thick lulling rhythm of the voice as the hands stroked and not listen and not care. It was easy that way except for the waves of loathing that would not stay back.

"You'll kiss your father good night?"

The lips closed and breath went as his arms crushed, now the repulsion of the mad flesh crushing in the struggle for breath.

"Good night, sleep well," he said and it was unimaginable relief to be free and to suck breath in and to wipe his track off the lips.

"Good night, Daddy."

"Good night, my son. Go to sleep now."

There was no hope of sleep, though soon the heavy breathing told that Mahoney had moved almost immediately into sleep. It was impossible to lie close. The loathing was too great. He lay far out on the bed's edge, but as Mahoney moved in his sleep all the clothes began to be dragged away, gathering in a huge ball around Mahoney, till only a sheet was left to cover him out on the bed's edge. It was bitterly cold and the loathing had soon to perish in the cold. He had to draw close to the sleeping heap of warmth. He tried to ease the clothes out from underneath the great body, but it needed too much force, it was too risky—he might wake. Not even whimpering could pass the time for long. The loud ticking of the clock filled the room when that stopped. As light grew its face would grow clear, it'd be possible to read the figures, but that was too far away in this cold under the single linen sheet. He tried again to free some clothes and the eiderdown came. He could bear it now. Though he'd give anything he had for one more blanket or the morning yet. Lunatic hatred rose choking against the restless sleeping bulk in the ball of blankets, the stupid bulk that had no care for anything except itself.

The bats screeched continually round the eaves outside. Morning got closer, and the fleas were biting. One was feeding on his shoulder. He tried to crush blindly down with his hand but it was no use. At least they were at his father too, that was why the bulk sleeping in the pile of blankets was so restless, other nights he slept like a log. They'd wake him yet. He was trying to scratch in his sleep. The fleas were having a real feast. He'd have to wake soon, and soon he did, an arm tearing itself free of the blankets.

"Are you sleeping?"

"No."

"Do you find anything?"

"I think the fleas are at it," he was able to keep the laugh back.

"I seem to be just one itch. They're going mad. The dose of DDT last month must have done no good."

He got out on the floor, found the box of matches, and lit the lamp on the table.

He dealt with his shirt first, taking it off, examining it inch by inch on the table. Each flea he found he kept it pressed under his hand till it was dead or exhausted. He'd catch it between both thumb-nails then, where it cracked utterly out of life, a red speck of skin and blood crushed on the nail.

The hunt started, five fleas in the sheets lively and hard to nail, but the blankets were easier, the fleas there warm and lazy with blood in the wool. The thumb-nails were easily brought to bear, there was no danger of the lightning hop free, they were too drugged, and one movement crushed them into another red speck in their sleep.

"If we don't get our death out of this we'll be alright," Mahoney said when it was over. "Sixteen fleas in the bed. We'll just have to get boxes of DDT and fumigate the whole house tomorrow. Do you think you'll be able to go to sleep now?"

"I'll be able to sleep."

Mahoney's eyes caught the red on his own thumb-nails as

he turned to quench the lamp. He brought them closer in fascination, bending his hair dangerously into the heat of the lamp.

"Your blood and mine," Mahoney said. "Those bastards feeding all the night on our blood. The quicker we get the DDT the better. Just think of it—those bastards feeding all the night on your blood and mine."

He blew out the flame and got into bed. The heavy blankets were marvellous and warm after. There was no repulsion as their flesh touched deep down in the clothes. There was no care of anything any more.

"Try and get some sleep, it'll be soon morning."

"Good night, Daddy."

"Good night. Try and get some sleep like a good man."

4

FATHER GERALD CAME EVERY YEAR, HE WAS A COUSIN AND HIS coming was a kind of watch. Mahoney hated it, but because of his fear of a priest's power he made sure to give the appearance of a welcome.

The front room was dusted and swept, the calico covers removed from the armchairs. A fire burned in the grate from early morning. A hen was killed and cooked for cold chicken, the set of wedding china unrolled out of the protective sheets in the bottom of the press. Though even in the lamplight and the friendly hissing of logs on the fire, the cloth bleached in the frost white as snow on the table, the room remained lifeless as any other good example.

"What do you want to be in the world?" the priest asked as the evening wore.

"I don't know, father. Whatever I'm let be I suppose."

"That's good truth out of your mouth for once," Mahoney asserted. "It's not what you want to be, it's what you'll be let be. He'll be like me I suppose. He'll wear out his bones on the few acres round this house and be buried at the end of the road."

"We'll be all buried," the priest insisted with an icy coldness, and it made the father crazy to do some violence.

"I sincerely hope so," he'd no care left whether he concealed his hatred or not any more. "It's some comfort to know that if you're not buried for love's sake you'll be buried for the stink's sake at any rate."

A flush coloured in the priest's pale and sunken cheeks but he stayed calm.

"He may not have to slave on any farm. He's been always head of his class."

"I was head of my class once too and far it got me."

"Times have changed. There are openings and opportunities today that never were before."

"I don't see them if there is, you can go to England, that's all I see."

He'd not be like his father if he could. He'd be a priest if he got the chance, and there were dreams of wooden pulpits and silence of churches, walking between yew and laurel paths in prayer, an old house with ivy and a garden, orchards behind. He'd walk that way through life towards the unnamable heaven of joy, not his father's path. He'd go free in God's name.

"Don't worry. Work at your books at school and we'll see what happens," the priest said as he shook hands at the gate.

"Work at your books," the father mimicked as his car left. "They're free with plans for other people's money, not their own. There he goes. Christmas comes but once a year."

He worked through the winter as hard as he was able and in summer won a scholarship to the Brothers' College. There wasn't much rejoicing.

25

"Take it if you want and don't take it if you don't want. It's your decision. I won't have you blaming me for the rest of your life that the one chance you did get that I stood in your way. Do what you want to do."

He knew Mahoney wanted him to stay from school and work in the fields.

"I'll take it," he said in spite of what he knew.

"Take it so and may it choke you but I'll not have you saying in after years that I kept you from it."

"I'll go," he said and he knew he was defying Mahoney, some way he'd be made pay for it.

A second-hand bicycle was got and fixed up. In September he started.

He hadn't long to wait for trouble. The new subjects didn't leave him much time to give the help in the fields Mahoney had been used to. There was constant trouble, it rose to a warning when he refused to stop for the potato digging.

"I can't. I'll miss too much. Once you fall behind it's too hard to catch up."

"Go but I'm warning you that what I dig must be off the ridges before night."

"I'll be home quick. The evenings are long enough yet."

"That's your business. But I'm warning you it'll be your own funeral if they're not off the ridges before night."

The first two evenings they were able to have the ridges cleared before dark. Mahoney seemed disappointed. He kept complaining, he wanted trouble, and he had only to wait for the next evening to get his chance. It came stormy, the sky a turmoil of black shifting cloud, and the wind so strong on the open parts of the road that not even stepping on the pedals could force the bike much faster than walking pace. The others were afraid in the kitchen when he came home late.

"Our father's wild. We'll never get what he's dug picked before night," they were afraid.

It started to rain as he gulped his meal, the first drops loud on the pane, and it was raining steadily by the time they were on their way to the field.

Between the lone ash trees, their stripped branches pale as human limbs in the rain, Mahoney worked. The long rows of the potatoes stretched to the stone wall, the rows washed clean on top by the rain, gleaming white and pink and candle-yellow against the black acres of clay; and they had to set to work without any hope of picking them all. Their clothes started to grow heavy with rain. The wind numbed the side of their faces, great lumps of clay held together by dead stalks gathered about their boots.

Yet Mahoney would not leave off. He paid no attention to them. He had reached close to the stone wall and he was muttering and striking savagely with the spade as he dug.

"He'll never leave off now. There's no knowing what he'll do," it was Joan.

"It doesn't matter. It doesn't matter at all."

Then they saw him come, blundering across the muddy ridges.

"Give me the bucket in the name of Jesus. Those bloody spuds'll not pick themselves."

He heaped fistfuls of mud into the bucket with the potatoes, in far too great a rush, and the bucket overturned and scattered his picking back on the ridge. He cursed and started to kick the bucket.

"Nothing right. Nothing right. Nothing ever done right. All lost in this pissin mess."

The blue shirt was plastered to his body under the army braces and showed naked. They thought he was going to go for them.

"I'll get me death out of this. Such cursed yokes to be saddled with. No help, no help," he turned to the rain instead.

27

"I'll get me death out of this pissin mess," he cursed as he went stumbling over the ridges to the house.

"That itself is one good riddance," was the harsh farewell after him in the rain.

They went on picking but it was hopeless, the dark was thickening. They were walking on the potatoes.

"We're only tramping them into the ground, Joan."

"But he'll murder us if we stop."

"Let him murder. We can pick no more. We'll have to cover the heap before we go in, that's all."

"But I'm afraid."

"It's alright. I'll tell him when I go in. There's no need to be afraid."

"I don't want to go in," it was Mona.

"It's not the end of the world, you know, they're only bloody spuds when all is said."

But why had things to happen as they did, why could there not be some happiness, it'd be as easy.

"As I was going to the fair of Athy I met nine men and their nine wives, how many were going to the fair of Athy?"

"Only the one, the rest were coming."

"Aren't you clever now of the County Roscommon?" and they were beginning to laugh.

They had to tidy still the face of the pit and it looked strange no matter what. The long pyramid sloped palely upwards to the edge, the sides washed white, gleaming blobs of flesh in the rain. They covered it with the green rushes, and weighed them down with shovelfuls of clay.

"God, O God, O God," they started to mimic, it was an old game between them, it brought relief.

"In the County Home you'll finish up and don't say then that your father didn't warn you."

"Wilful waste is woeful want. God, O God, O God."

It was very dark, the wind had risen, sweeping walls of

rain across the fields. Some of the last leaves fell lightly against them as they came through the orchard. He had the lamp lit and no blinds down, so they made straight for its yellow tunnel into the night, brilliants of the raindrops flashing through.

Mahoney sat in his dry clothes in the kitchen. The fire was blazing, traces of his eaten meal were on the table, he was more tired than angry, but he felt he had to squash the accusation of them standing there in dripping clothes.

"Did you pick them all?"

"No."

"They'll be in a grand state if the frost comes."

"I never saw frost and rain together."

"Did you not now? You're bound to know all about it too, aren't you, and you going to college too."

There was no attempt to answer, but Mahoney did nothing, only kept complaining.

"And did you cover the pit itself?"

"We did—with the rushes."

"I suppose you'll be expecting a leather medal for that much," he jeered.

The only answer was a curse under the breath, and a turning to the room to change, to break into a fit of weeping, the hands gripping the brass railing of the bed going white. When he was calm enough to change and come down Mahoney was still nagging wearily in the kitchen.

Even he had to tire and stop sometime and when he did the uneasiness grew if anything deeper in the silence where they listened to the overflow from the tar barrels spill out on the flagstones of the street.

29

5

ONE DAY SHE WOULD COME TO ME, A DREAM OF FLESH IN
woman, in frothing flimsiness of lace, cold silk against my
hands.

An ad. torn from the *Independent* by my face on the
pillow, black and white of a woman rising. Her black lips open
in a yawn. The breasts push out the clinging nightdress she
wears, its two thin white straps cross her naked shoulders.
Her arms stretch above her head to bare the growths of hair
in both armpits.

REMOVE SUPERFLUOUS HAIR

The eyes devour the tattered piece of newspaper as hotness
grows. Touch the black hair with the lips, salt of sweat same
as my own, let them rove along the rises of the breast. Press
the mouth on the black bursting lips, slip the tongue through
her teeth. Go biting along the shoulder over the straps to the

dark pits again. She stirs to life, I have her excited, she too is crazy, get hands under her. One day she must come to me. I try to pump madly on the mattress, fighting to get up her nightdress, and get into her, before too late, swoon of death into the softness of her flesh. One day, one day, one day rising to a breaking wave, and that shivering pause on the height before the seed pulses, and the lips kiss frantically on the pillow.

"I love you, I love you, oh my love, I love you to the end of the world, my love."

The pulsing dies away, a last gentle fluttering, and I can lie quiet. The day of the room returns, red shelves with the books and the black wooden crucifix, the torn piece of newspaper on the pillow. Everything is dead as dirt, it is as easy to turn over. I'd committed five sins since morning.

The first time it had only been a matter of pressing, just time to get on the sock before it spilled out into the sheets, the second was easy too, but after that it was resort to the imagination: Mary Moran's thighs working against the saddle of the bicycle as she came round by Kelly's of the Big Park with a can of milk, the whiteness and hairs of Mrs. Murphy's legs above the canvas shoes in summer, and silk and all sorts of lace. Nylons from Cassidy's stretched on round thighs in the *Independent* and REMOVE SUPERFLUOUS HAIR, it had to be concentrate and use imagination then.

Five sins already today, filthiness spilling five times, but did it matter, the first sin was as damning as a hundred and one, but five sins a day made thirty-five in a week, they'd not be easy to confess.

Bless me, father, for I have sinned. It's a month since my last Confession. I committed one hundred and forty impure actions with myself.

A shudder started at what the priest would say.

"One hundred and forty impure actions with yourself, my child?"

31

Flushed cheeks was all that was left to show what I had done, and the sock. Pull it off, the wool was wet, but it'd dry. Only for the discovery once of the sock's uses the sheet would stain grey and stiff as with starch and Mahoney might notice.

The clock beat on the lowest of the shelves, twenty past three. A great clattering army of stares were black on the yew tree outside the window, and it was time to get up and dress and go downstairs.

"No care for your shoes. Wear away. And this old fool can sit on his arse all day and fix them, O God, O God," I could hear as I came down.

He was mending boots, the old brown apron over his lap, Joan in attendance, and the hours I stood there in the same way as she stood, the solid misery and boredom of it.

"It was sprigs I wanted; not tacks, you fool. The stupidity of this house," and the one thing worth waiting for was to see the hammer come down on his thumb and watch him dance and suck.

The boots were bargain boots from the Autumn Sale in Curleys, always a size too large in case our feet would grow. The strips of bicycle tyre across the sole couldn't keep them from wearing for very long, and then it was wear them down to the uppers rather than have to listen to his nagging. At night they'd have to be hidden, but if he was suspicious he'd hunt them out, the rack of lying up in bed listening to him hunting for the boots downstairs.

"Anything but tell. Wear them away and let the old fool pay. Money comes down in a shower of rain," was the tune, and joy to fling them away in April and go barefoot on the grass, Bruen's paddocks with a can for mushrooms, and into the whole of summer to October.

"So you managed to get up, did you? Miracles will never cease."

"I'm alright. I'll go to school Monday."

"And get a relapse and more doctors?"

"I'm alright."

"Everyone's all right and this old fool has nothing to do but fix!"

I could do little but get books and bury myself in them at the fire, he'd resent that, but he couldn't do much more.

A Memoriam card slipped out of the first book. A black tassel hung from its centre, miniature of her wedding photo glued to the cardboard. Her small face was beautiful, the mass of chestnut hair. The white wedding dress drooped away from her throat. She was smiling.

"Pray for the soul of," and it took iron effort to keep back the rush of grief.

Eternal rest grant unto her, O Lord.
And let perpetual light shine upon her.
And may she rest in peace. Amen.

On the road as I came with her from town loaded with parcels and the smell of tar in the heat I'd promised her that one day I'd say Mass for her. And all I did for her now was listen to Mahoney's nagging and carry on private orgies of abuse.

I'd never be a priest. I was as well to be honest. I'd never be anything. It was certain.

There was little to do but sit at the fire and stare out at the vacancy of my life at sixteen.

6

MUCH OF THE WORST IN THE HOUSE HAD SHIFTED TOWARDS THE others, you had your own room with the red shelves after long agitation, you had school and books, you were a growing man.

There had only been one heavy beating in the year, a time over a shocking absurdity with cotton wool and a corset far too tight for Joan when her first flow of blood came to her, but it was less possible to stand and watch him beat the others, and much of the fear of him was going. He was frozen out. He had to play patience alone all the time, and as he felt his power go in the house he took fits of brute assertion, carried away by rage and suspicions, and it was only a matter of time till there'd be a last clash.

He came in crazy to do someone after tripping over a bucket he'd left carelessly behind him in the darkness. He picked "ALWAYS" out of a conversation over by the sewing-machine. He was crazy with frustration.

"Did I hear you mention ALWAYS?" he attacked in a savage voice and the girls turned afraid.

"Did you know that there's only one thing you should use ALWAYS about and that's God. He always was and always will be, for ever and ever, Amen," he shouted, half-frothing already with the force of the nonsense rhetoric. "Did you know that?"

"No."

"What were you talking about?"

"We were just saying it'd be always like this," and they looked so afraid that it roused his suspicion. They'd been talking about him, their hopeless life with no sign of change. It'd be always as this.

"The weather," Joan said but it was plain she was lying, and he pounced, gripping her by the shoulder and hair.

"No. It was not. Out with the truth. Before it's too late—I'll not give you a second chance."

"We said it'd be always like this, in this house."

"This house," he repeated. "This house. It'll be always like this. So you're not satisfied, it's not grand enough for you, is it not? Not for lying and throwing buckets out of your hand for people to kill themselves across."

He swung her by the hair. Her feet left the ground. He started to swing her round by the dark hair, mouthing, "I'll teach you to lie. Talk about people behind their backs. I'll teach you to lie," and she was screaming.

You'd watched it come to this, hatred rising with every word and move he made, but you'd watched so many times it was little more than habit. Then her heels left the ground and swung, the eyes staring wide with terror out of the face, and the screaming. You couldn't bear any more this time.

"Stop it. Stop it, I tell you."

35

Mahoney stopped as if struck, she fell in a heap on the floor, though he did not loose his grip of the hair.

"What did you say?"

"I said to stop it, let her go," and you couldn't control the trembling. Mahoney let go the hair and she slumped on the floor. With one savage bound and swing he sent you hurtling against the table, you felt the wood go hard into the side, but no pain, it was almost a kind of joy. You came back from the table and able to shout, "Hit," as he came.

He did hit, swinging his open palm with his whole strength across the face, and this time you went sideways to crash against the dresser.

You didn't even feel the white knob drive into your side. You were mad with strength, coming off the dresser like a reflex.

"Hit and I'll kill you," you said and you knew nothing, there was no fear, you watched the hand come up to hit, your own hands ready and watching the raised hand and the throat. You knew or felt nothing, except once the raised hand moved you'd get him by the throat, you knew you'd be able, the fingers were ready. No blow could shake you, only release years of stored hatred into that one drive for the throat.

Mahoney fell back without striking, as if he sensed, mixture of incomprehension and fear on the face. The world was a shattered place.

"I reared a son that'd lift a hand to his father. A son that'd lift a hand to his father."

"Do you see her hair still in your fingers?" Some of the tautness had gone, you wouldn't attack now, but there was more than enough violence left.

He had to look. Strands of her black hair were tangled in his fingers. By spreading them he thought the hair would fall loose but it didn't.

"I reared a son that'd lift a hand to his father."

36

The sudden strength of madness that had come was now draining rapidly away.

"Get up, Joan," you stooped to get her to her feet and help her to the big armchair. The others stood as stones about. They knew that something strange and different had happened in the house.

"Get her a drink of water," you asked and one of the girls obeyed as decisively as if you were Mahoney and you didn't care or know.

"You'd hit your father?"

"You wouldn't swing a pig like that."

"I'd swing anyone that way, you too. Pigs. The whole lot of you are pigs, a vicious litter of pigs. It's the whip I should have given the whole lot of you."

"You'll give no one the whip," and you were drained and sick of it all.

"So you'll stop it. You'll be the hero now. Come on, try it, hit your father, the pup is stronger than the dog. Come on, my pup, and try it."

You hadn't the strength even if you'd wanted. The whole kitchen and world was sick and despairing. Hatred had drained everything empty.

"No. I'll not hit."

"But you would hit. You'd lift a hand to your father only for you're too yellow, that's all that's keeping you back. And you're the one that goes to school too, the makings of the priest. A fine young cuckoo they'll have then. A priest, no less, and saying Mass and everything," he laughed.

The violence had been easier far than the jeering and mockery.

"You'd more than a year's luck on your side that you didn't hit," Mahoney went on asserting. "I'd have smashed you to pieces, do you hear that, to pieces, you pup, and you'd have tried it, you pup."

"You can hit away. Batter and beat away as you always did. No one cares any more."

Mahoney kept taunting, moving to the fire, where he disentangled the hairs out of his fingers, and let them drop into the flames. The silence of some horror came at last when they sizzled there as flesh.

You went outside into the night, clean with stars, but you didn't linger; but went by the plot of great rhubarb stalks to the dark lavatory, refuge of many evenings.

7

ABOUT THE CONFESSION BOXES THE QUEUES WAITED, DARK IN their corners, the centre of the church the one place lighted, red glow of the lamp high before the tabernacle and the candles in their sockets burning above the gleaming brass of the shrine. Beads rattled, bodies eased their positions. Feet came in down at the door, step after step tolling on the stones as they neared the rails to genuflect before the tabernacle and turn to the boxes in the dark corners, eyes on them till they were recognized in the tabernacle light. All waited for forgiveness, in the listless performance of habit and duty or torturing and turning over their sins and lives, time now to judge themselves and beg, on the final day there would be neither time nor choice.

Through the sacristy door the priests come, they kneel before the altar, kiss and don the purple stole of their office as they move out to the boxes through the gate in the wooden rails. You can hear your heart beating as the shutter rattles open on the first penitent. In fear and shame you are moving to the death of having to describe the real face of your life to your God in his priest, and to beg forgiveness, and promise, for there is still time.

There was an even flow that carried you nearer. You were sick and wanted to leave but you couldn't. You tried to grasp in the memory your sins once more: lies four times, anger three, prayers not said five or six or eight times it hardly mattered. Sins of lust after women every day in your mind for the last three months, orgies of self-abuse, the mind flinched from admitting the exact number of times, two hundred times or more. You were steadily moving in the flow of the queue towards a confession of guilt, and the moment of confessing would be a kind of death.

Was the flow of time towards the hour of his execution different for the man in the condemned cell in Mountjoy? Vain effort of the cards and wardens to distract him through the night and then on the hour Pierrepoint and his two assistants come and it's still not real and they are marching to Pierrepoint's time. There'll be strict formality and order now.

"Left, right. Left, right. Turn to the left. Mark time.

"Are you ready, sir?" Pierrepoint asks and moving to time the assistants handcuff the condemned hands behind.

"Follow me, sir," Pierrepoint's voice in the cell of his life for the last time and they go marching, "Left, right. Left, right. Left, right," to the scaffold, the priest walking by his side and praying too in time,

"O, Jesus, who for love of me didst bear thy cross to Calvary, in thy sweet mercy grant to me to suffer and to die with thee. O, Jesus, who for love of me didst bear thy cross to Calvary, in thy sweet mercy grant to me to suffer and to die with thee."

40

Here you'd only to move nearer in the queue and when it got to your turn draw the heavy curtain aside, no scream at the sight of the scaffold, and kneel in the darkness and wait. Though was it any different, were all waitings not the same, was it any different except in the sensitivity, the intensity.

The slide rattled open. Through the wire grille you saw the sideface inclined towards you.

"Bless me, father, for I have sinned," the time had come and though you could hardly force the words out it was still the dreadful moment.

"How long is it since your last confession?"

"Three months, father."

"Now tell me your sins, my child."

"I told lies four times. I was angry three times. Eight or nine times I didn't say my prayers——"

"Anything else, my child?"

It would be so easy to answer, "No, father. Nothing else," but that would be worse than anything.

"Yes, father," you didn't know how you were able to admit it.

"Confess then, my child. You needn't be afraid."

"I had impure thoughts and did impure actions."

"Were these impure actions with yourself or someone else?"

"With myself, father."

"You deliberately excited yourself?"

"Yes, father."

"Did you cause seed to come?"

"Yes, father."

"How many times?"

"Sometimes seven or eight times a day and other times not at all, father."

"Could you put a number on them?"

"More than two hundred times."

"And the thoughts?"

41

"More times than the actions, father," it was all out now, one pouring river of relief.

"That is all you have to tell, my child?"

"That's all, father."

"You must fight that sin, it'll grip you like a habit if you don't, if you don't break it now you may never be able to break it. You must come often to confession. Never let yourself stay away more than a month. Come every week if you can. You must pray for grace. You must make up your mind to break that sin once and for all now, tonight. Confession is worthless if you're not firmly decided on that."

"I promise, father."

Such relief had come to you, fear and darkness gone, never would you sin again. The pleasures seemed so mean and grimy against the sheer delight of peace, pure as snow in the air.

"For your penance say a rosary before the Blessed Sacrament."

The hand was raised in absolution, with almost ecstasy you breathed out the poor words of the Contrition:

"O my God, I am heartily sorry for having offended thee and I detest my sins above every other evil——"

"God bless you. Say a prayer for me, my child," and the world was woken by the banging across of the wooden shutter, just wire and wood before you now, the smell of cloves.

Dazed, you got up, and pulled aside the curtain. The world was unreal. All your life had been gathered into the Confession, it had been lost, it was found. O God, how beautiful the world was. The benches, the lamps, the people kneeling there, all washed in wonder, the sheer quiet mystery of their faces. How beautiful the world was, you wanted to say to them, and why did they not dance and smile back at you, sing and praise. Why did the candles in the candle-shrine not flame and dance, why didn't the benches pound and dance,

42

awkward wood dancing, and could the peoples' hands not clap time.

Perhaps it was enough to know it was so and go quietly to an empty bench up the church and kneel and hide your face in trembling hands. There was such joy. You were forgiven, the world given back to you, washed clean as snow. You'd never sin again. The world was too beautiful a place to lose. You willed yourself to say the rosary, wanting new words that never were before. Afterwards, even in the very pitch of the coughing and shuffling, there were remote areas of pure silence to pray and wander in eternally.

You started with fright when your arm was touched, it was your father, and how in a moment one wave of violent hatred came choking over prayer and silence.

"You can't be long more. I'll wait for you out at the gate," he leaned close to whisper.

You watched him away, he genuflected in the bloody glow of the sanctuary lamp, his head was bowed. What did he know whether you'd be long or short, you might pray all night yet, what did he know, and now he was waiting at the gate in the cold. And death shall have no dominion, rang in hatred and without reason in your mind.

You were in the state of grace, you remembered you were supposed to love everyone, and your father was waiting for you outside at the gate. You had no right to hate him, he was there to be loved too. So you mechanically rose, genuflected where he had genuflected and so many before both of you, and walked outside.

8

HE WAS WAITING AT THE GATE, PACING ABOUT IN THE COLD, examining the lost things that hung from the spikes.

"It's a good job people's arses are well tied on to them in this country or they'd leave them behind every time they sat down," he remarked laughing by way of greeting.

They walked together, breaking time to avoid the pot-holes filled with water, where again and again a star shivered.

"It's a great feeling after Confession. You feel everything's put right. You have no cares any more," Mahoney said.

"No. You have no cares," he agreed, though loathing the direction of the words. He had his own joy. He didn't want it confused in the generality of another's confession. There never had been understanding or anything. But he was troubled by the intensity of the hatred, they were commanded

44

to love, though the nerves bristled with hate at every advance or contact.

"Have you ever decided what you'll be when you grow up?"

"It depends on the exams mostly. Whatever I get. There's not much use in thinking."

Though he'd felt this night that he might be able to be a priest, a real priest, the one thing that was worth being. He'd felt he might be about good enough.

"Exams," he heard Mahoney. "By the columns of names these days in the *Independent* it appears that half the country will have passed an exam for something or other soon. Passed to ate one another if you ask me, for where'll the jobs come outa? Only the ones with the pull will get the jobs. I know what I'm talking about."

"Pull doesn't count in some of them. Not for the University Scholarship nor the call to train for a teacher or the E.S.B. And there's always England," was said harshly.

"No, I didn't mean that. We all know any fool can go to England once he gets his hands on a fiver. I didn't mean that. I know you've had it in your head to be a priest so I was just wondering what you intended to try to be," the voice was gentle enough for once, upset by the harshness of, There's always England. There was the temptation to be easy, not to keep him always outside, and the longing to confide, the world on your own was a cold place.

"I often think I might, if I could be good enough."

"I guessed as much myself. It's a good life and a clean one and you don't have bostoons trying to sit on you as in most jobs. God's your boss."

"You'd be all reared then and I could sell the old land and come to live with you. I could open the door for those calling and find out what they wanted and not have them annoying you about everything. I could fool around the garden, and

45

the bit of orchard at the back. We could bring the old tarred boat and go fishing in the summer."

That was his dream, but there was no response. He grew aware of his own voice and stopped. He'd be given nothing. The dream was not the other's dream. Perhaps too much had happened or lives were never meant to meet. The eagerness left his walk, he was let seem foolish to himself, and broken. No response came. Not even when he placed his hand on the shoulder that was now almost tall as his own.

"If it happened that you did, we'd have good times that way, wouldn't we?"

"We would. We'd have good times."

"What do you think the chances are that you'll go on?"

"I don't know. It's too hard to know. It depends on too many things."

9

THE LINE OF BLACK CATTLE TRAILED ALL THAT WINTER ROUND the fields in search of grass, only small patches in the shelter; always a funeral of little winter birds in their wake in the hope that the rocking hooves would loosen the frozen earth down to the worms. And in the evenings they'd crowd at the gate to low with steaming breaths for their fodder.

No rain came, a cloudless Easter, and a cloudless May, grass no higher in the fenced-off meadows than in the pastures, the young oats stunted, the apple blossoms scorched in nights of white frost.

When it broke it was too late in June: the quick unhealthy growths the sudden rains brought infested the cattle with worms, and it was a struggle to survive, anxiety and senseless recrimination never far away.

"It'll be the poor-house. I'm saddled with such lazy misfortunate bastards, we'll have the poor-house anyhow, something to look forward to at the end of our days when we expect some ease and respect. God, O God, O God."

Joan and Mona had left National School and were about the house. Mahoney decided in that pinching autumn to send Joan out into the world.

She'd become a common drudge since leaving school but the prospect of a job brought her no pleasure. She cried by the window the first night it was mentioned. She saw the same drudgery everywhere and what she knew was less to be feared than what she didn't.

Mahoney tried the newspapers first, but they yielded nothing, and in the end he had to write in chagrin to Father Gerald, who got her a job in a draper's shop near where he was curate.

He called to collect her and the usual preparations greeted his coming into an evening as lifeless and as starched as always. The conversation people make to avoid each other went shuttlecock for two agonized hours, before Mahoney made excuse to get out.

"We'll leave the lad and yourself together, father. You might have things to talk about, school and that, together. We'll look after Joan's getting ready and leave you alone."

The room apologetically emptied, they were alone.

"So the first bird is leaving the nest?" the priest said.

What was there to do but nod in vague depression, she was going, all departures touched in some way everyone's departure, became disturbing echoes.

"You'll not feel till your own turn?"

"No, father."

"You have no final inkling of what you might do yet?"

"No. It'll depend on the exams."

"Do you still think of the priesthood?"

"Yes, father, if I could be good enough."

48

"It was a great pity you were never sent to the Diocesan Seminary, the time your father wanted you to stay at home from school altogether."

"But there's the Mission Colleges?"

"Yes, but as a last resort. They do good work but the fact remains that they class you with the second-raters for Africa. But if you do very well in the Leaving it may be possible to get you even into Maynooth."

He smiled in reflection, "Doors open under the right pressures. We are cousins. And if we cannot help our own who can we help! But don't worry, all you can profitably do now is work hard at your studies. Perhaps next year you can come and stay with me for part of the summer holidays, and we can talk properly then?"

"Thank you, father."

"That's settled then, it's late, we could find the others and go—I hate driving in the late night, it gets so hard to keep eyes on the road!"

They found Mahoney idle with the others in the kitchen, Joan ready to leave, and they left immediately. There was something breaking at the priest's car in the way she kissed them good-bye, Mahoney visibly disturbed as he stooped into the smell of brilliantine that damped her dark hair.

"We'll write. We'll write. Take care of yourself," he said.

They opened the green gates for the car and watched the headlights search into the hills before they were lost.

He was restless when he came in, pacing about. He started to cram the bits of twine scattered about the house into an empty tea-box.

"Scattered everywhere about, no care, nothing ever done right in the house."

He got boards and stood them on their ends against the kitchen wall, and laid one across two chairs for planing. The

49

plane wasn't sharp enough; so on the black bone wet with bicycle oil he sharpened it and complained.

Soon he was in his shirt-sleeves, the kitchen too warm, beads of sweat glistened as he drove the plane over and back, the long white shavings littering the floor. He didn't finish. He'd no interest once this savage need to do was exhausted.

"Sweep up the shavings, they'll make kindling," he said, and he pulled the old Morris car seat up to the fire, its red leather faded, in the wooden frame he'd made for it. He put on his coat and got the pack of cards and playing-board. He sat and laid the playing-board across the unpainted arms of the frame. As he began he looked suddenly an infant enclosed in its pen chair.

The others stood as sentinels about or went outside. Joan was gone, a breath of death in the air, Mahoney was playing, nothing in the silence but his lonely playing, the shuffling of the deck, swish of the sharp boxing together, as he dealt them out on the board those worn cards of patience flicking. The yellow cat stretched in the ashes. A low pursing came from his lips as he deliberated where each card would best fit. King of Diamonds for the Ace, Eight of Clubs for the Nine, the Seven by lucky chance for the Eight. He gathers together again what is left. Three by three he counts them out on the unpainted playing-board, red and black, from count to count till no move is left. He gathers them all violently into a heap to begin the journey over again to the same dead end or to reach what he'd been playing for, all the cards magically leaping to their ordered places, once in every four or five hundred times—long lighthouse patience.

"Look, it's come out," he could shout, or gloat in secret. Nothing came near out and he was too restless.

"What was your beloved cousin talking about?" he asked.

"Not much."

"Not much—such a bloody answer. So the pair of you

50

stood and gaped at each other with your mouths open."

"No."

"What did he say so?"

"He said about being a priest."

"What did he say about that?"

"He said he'd help, and not to worry. He said that nothing could be done till after the exams."

"He meant he'd buy the calf when it was reared a bullock?"

"No, no, he didn't mean that. He said he'd help. He said he might be able to get me into Maynooth."

"Maynooth, no less. Doesn't it cost money to get into Maynooth?"

"It does."

"He didn't say who was going to do the paying, did he?"

"No. He didn't say."

"Believe me he didn't. He's very free with money not his own."

"He said he'd help and no one said I might be a priest at all yet, who knows?"

"What did he say about Joan?" Mahoney changed.

"He said nothing."

"I suppose he thinks I should have brought her up to be better than a shop girl."

"He didn't say what he thought."

"Believe me he didn't say what he thought. He's far too clever for that."

His face was heated, the lines of the mouth moving. The eyes were tired and hunted. He brought up his old boots that were wet from driving the cattle through the rushes, and put them by the fire to dry. He unlaced the new boots he'd worn for the priest.

"It's not what people say that counts, it's what they think. If you ever want to get on in the world don't heed what they say but find out what's going on in their numbskulls. That's what'll get you on.

"Think what you say but don't say what you think and then you have some chance but what do I care. They can think themselves into the Sligo madhouse for all I care," he shouted.

The wool of his socks whispered on the cement as he went to the door.

"Go to your beds before long, I'm dead out, and don't forget to quench the lamp."

10

EACH WEEK A LETTER CAME FROM JOAN—D.V. AFTER HER hopes, and S.A.G. on the back of the blue envelope, as she'd been piously taught to put at National School. Each was written to the same wooden formula, nothing of herself or life let come through. She hoped this letter found them as well as it left her. So they assumed that she was at least reasonably happy.

Violence seldom flared any more, Mahoney didn't seem to care so much, mostly complaining or absorbed in tired introspection.

As the struggle outside eased it grew worse within the skull. You could get no control. You'd go weeks without committing any sin, in often ecstatic prayer and sense of God, again replaced by weeks of orgy sparked by a fit of simple boredom or unhappiness. The constant effort back to Confession, haunted by the repetitive hypocrisy of your life, anguish of the struggle towards repeated failure. Time was running out too. You had to spend the coming summer with Father Gerald. He'd expect you to have reached some decision. The winter after would be the last year of your life at school.

No ecstasy after Confession any more. You were able to kneel and stare out of the protecting darkness into the blood-red glow before the altar, the same penances to say, the same promises of amendment, and how long would it last, a month or a week or days? You'd no control over your lusts and if you hadn't how could you stay a priest?

A priest on a Saturday night in your own smell in the confession box listening to a month of pleasure and sin and would you be able to stay calm while a girl told about a night in June, fragrance of her perfume mixed with sweat as sweet as roses on the altar, rustle of her taffeta, and the moon above the evergreens outside the windows.

"Bless me, father, for I have sinned."

"Tell me your sins, my child."

"I was guilty of impure actions, father."

"With a man, my child?"

"Yes, father."

"Was he married or single?"

"Single, father."

"You're not engaged to him?"

"No, father."

"Tell me what happened, my child."

"Passionate kissing and embracing, father."

"Were you touched, my child?"

"Yes, father."

"On the breasts?"

"Yes, father."

"In another sacred place as well?"

"Yes, father."

"How or where did this happen?"

"In the river meadows, after the marquee dance in the Golf Club."

"Did you actually have intercourse with this man, my child?"

A whimper of grief in her voice, her dress would rustle, her face and young body close as inches to yours in the night. The same young thighs that had opened submissively wide to the man's rise the summer's night by the river might open wide as that for you. She'd give you the fulfilment you craved. You'd have known pleasure before you died, it seemed a great deal to know. Bread might be marvellous in starvation, you'd find total meaning in devouring it for the time of hunger, but your hunger was for a woman, mirage of total marvel and everything in her flesh.

And what would you do? Stay quiet and begin, "Don't you know, my child, that you are only permitted to do these things in Holy Matrimony. You must avoid places and temptations to that sin, you must promise me that."

Or would you sit quiet and excite your own seed in the box with your hand or pressing against the wood and let it flow in the darkness, same as Onan; her rustling clothes and voice and smell sweeping through the wire grille. Her flesh beyond the wire hungered too for its fodder, the thrusting body of a man for her own.

Or would you burst out of the box and take her in madness? She'd said she'd been a virgin. She'd cried out with hurt in the river meadows but the man would not stop, he took her against her will. Would she cry too when you the priest tore her clothes off and took her on the stone floor of the church?

That might be your priest's life, if you'd no control now was there chance it might be different then. At least you had a choice now to go out into the world and get women, but

55

once you were a priest you were a priest for ever, there'd be no choice left, and once you were trapped in your own choice would you stay quiet in it or go crazy? A priest all your days, hair coming away by its white roots on your comb till baldness and death, and never in all those days to have touched and entered the roused flesh of a woman in her heat, never for your nakedness to be hid in her nakedness, never to be held in her softness, buried deep in the darkness of her red flesh, and her hands stroking the nerves to ecstasy.

Where was fear of hell gone, scorched and frenzied bodies howling on steaming stones and irons through the boredom of eternity, the racks and tortures? All lives moved into death, the last taste in every mouth, and it wasn't sweet. Perhaps there was no final destruction on woman though it'd be dream always, just the death of passion, you'd have to crawl out same as after any orgy till it renewed, and the same circus of the flesh would pitch its tents again in another night of longing, nothing but this drifting death from hole to hole.

You'd master it as a priest. You'd give your life back to God, you'd serve, you'd go to death in God's name and not your own. You'd choose your death, you'd give up desire other than in God. You'd die into God the day of your ordination. All your life would be a death in readiness for the last moment when you'd part with your flesh and leave. You'd be safe. Even if there was no God or hell or heaven it didn't make much difference, every one was as poor and equal in death as every other, and you'd have possibly less sorrow, less remembered pleasure, for if the schooling was for nothing it was still schooling.

The more you lingered on it the more fantastic it grew, no open road, the best was to be a green cabbage head. Say your penance. Go as best you can till you fall, the refuge of confession again then, and it all had the saving grace that it wasn't going to last for ever.

Evenings after school you hung about the shops waiting for Mary Moran to pass down from the Convent, let her cycle out the road a little ahead, and pedal furiously to catch her round Clark's.

"How are you, Mary?"

"Oh, you gave me a fright."

"I thought you'd not be out yet and I got a surprise when I came round the turn and saw you ahead," you explained, though you'd waited for twenty minutes in the hammering of Gill's bicycle shop with eyes never off the road till she passed.

"No. We didn't delay around the Convent. I came straight. Don't you seem to be late?"

"We hung about the alley. The others are mostly there yet. Was there anything strange today?"

Her voice was pure music, it sent shivers of delight trembling. No one ever smiled as she did. A secret world was around her. Her thighs moved on the saddle, you got conscious of the friction of your own thighs, got roused, desperate in case she'd notice. Every bit of the road was precious, only it went so fast, so much to tell and to hear, and it was marvel, the world for the very first time. If you had twenty miles to travel it wouldn't be enough, and the four went past before you could hold or taste them and you were saying an impossible good-bye.

She was gone and dream of her took over, Mary and you together, and married. With her you'd walk a life as under the shade of trees, a life in a wild summer that'd last for ever.

But you couldn't even hold her pure, you took her into your mind a wet Saturday, excited her, put foul abuse in her mouth. Afterwards took the woollen sock that had soaked the seed and held it to the light.

"Fuck it," was said quiet, eyes on the wet stain, dust of tiredness or hopelessness dry in your mouth.

You couldn't have Mary Moran if you went to be a priest

57

and you couldn't be a priest as you were. The only way you could have her anyhow was as an old whore of your mind, and everything was growing fouled.

Summer came, the days closing on when you'd have to go to Father Gerald, Corpus Christi the last feast before.

The rhododendron branches were cut out of Oakport same as always to decorate the grass margins of the processional route, banners of red and gold stretched overhead from the telegraph poles with "O Sacred Heart of Jesus"; and the altars stood before the houses of the way, candles burning among the flowers, the picture of the Sacred Heart torn bleeding from its breast against the white linen.

Under the gold canopy the priest moved with the Sacrament, girls in their communion dresses strewing rose petals in its path, and behind the choir the banners of the sodalities self-conscious in the wake of the hymns. At the bridges and crossroads the police stood to salute.

Before the post office the people knelt in the dry dust of the road for Benediction. The humeral veil was laid on the priest's shoulders, the tiny bell tinkled in the open day, the host was raised and all heads bowed, utter silence except for the bell and some donkey braying in the distance. Kneeling in the dust among the huddled crowd it was hard to fight back tears. This was the way your life was, you belonged to these people, as they to you, you were linked together. One day that Sacred Host would be your burden to uphold for them while the bell rang, but it was still impossible to join in the singing as the procession resumed its way, only listen to the shuffle of boots through the dust. *Wash me ye waters streaming from His side*, it was strange, all strange, and the candles burning against the yew trees in the day.

Or was it all mere pomp and ceremony to cover up the unendurable mystery, the red petals withering in the centre of the road with the people drinking or gone home? It was impossible to know, and in that uncertainty you went to confession, you had to find some limbo of control before facing the priest, but you were farther from any decision or certainty than ever before in your life.

11

Cur non sub alta vel platano vel hac
pinu iacentes sic temere et rosa
   canos odorati capillos
   dum licet, Assyriaque nardo
potamus uncti? dissipat Euius
curas edaces.

THE ROCKING OF THE BUS JOGGED THE SMALL BLUE TEXTBOOK
in his hands as he read, writing first the meaning of the new
words on the margin after he'd looked up the vocabulary in
the back. Once he was sure of all the meanings he'd try to
translate.

Why should we not lie stretched carelessly under that pine-
tree or the tall plane, and scent our white hair with roses while
we may, and anointed with Syrian spikenard let us drink?
Bacchus drives eating cares away.

60

He was able to translate it. He lifted his eyes and smiled, whether from the satisfaction, it seemed to make meaning enough, or because it evoked a beautiful life and way—old men fragrant with roses drinking life heedlessly away under the plane tree.

He'd not be asked about beauty in the LEAVING next June. He'd be asked to translate it, to scan it, to comment on grammatical usages. Horace wasn't easy, he was for the *Honours*. So he laboured on mechanically through the notes and text.

Later he closed the book, his eyes tired from the print jogging before them. Outside the dusty windows of the bus a bright day in August was ending, the few women in the seats beginning to wear cardigans loose about the shoulders of their summer dresses.

Since midday he'd travelled in this reek of diesel and warm rubber and leather, an hour's wait in Cavan that he'd used to hang about the streets, football fever in the town, references in the passing salutations.

"If Peter Donoughue has his shooting boots on Cavan will win, though it'll be tight," a conductor with a green tin box in his hands said outside the waiting-room door, and it had for some reason stayed.

"Is it long more?" he turned and asked as he let the Latin textbook slip into his pocket.

"No. Not long. Eight or ten minutes."

"Thanks."

He stared ahead. Father Gerald would be waiting. In eight or ten minutes they'd meet, and the strange thing was that the whole decision and meeting had seemed closer and more definite six months before, the day the priest took Joan away. The nearer the waiting got to its end the more certain it seemed that it could never end, it must surely last for ever, though it was actually ending even now. A country town huddled beneath church spires was in sight, and the conductor nodded. He'd arrived. As the bus slowed he took his coat and case from the overhead rack and the black figure of the priest with Joan at his side grew recognizable out of the few people waiting on the pavement.

After the first greetings, the inquiries and answers about the journey, it was Father Gerald who told him that they'd been invited to tea in Ryans, where Joan worked. They went towards it down the street, O Riain in florid Celtic lettering on the draper's lintel. The shop was closed. They knocked on the hall door, up steps one side of the shop.

Mrs. Ryan welcomed them, a large woman with a mass of hair that must have been black once, her big body showing well out of the grey tweed dress. Three daughters and a son waited in the dining-room with their father. He seemed dominated in some way. She introduced them, one by one, shaking hands with father and son and bowing to the daughters with such strain that he was only half aware of what he was doing. They sat to the laden table. After the tea was poured the priest offered Grace.

The meal passed in continual pleasantry and gossip, even Ryan towards the end asserted himself enough to tell a safe joke. Afterwards they sat together till close to midnight, a kind of intensity or excitement gathering, whether from the closeness of bodies or personalities, for the local talk hardly deserved such eagerness or passion. The priest's face was flushed when he rose, he lingering for twenty minutes prolonging it between the chair and the door, reluctant to let the evening go, though it was past its time.

That was the one chance he got alone with Joan. She'd grown since she left them, but her face was more pale and drawn.

"Are you alright?"

She said nothing, he knew something was the matter.

"Are you not happy, Joan, or what?"

"No, it's worse than home," she said and that was all there was time for before they were joined by Mrs. Ryan.

"It's worse than home," troubled him in the priest's car but he had no time to hunt to see.

"We're late, strange how you hang too long talking once it goes late, anything rather than go home. And when you think back you can't know what you've been talking all the time about," the priest said as he drove fast into the empty night, the branches of the trees along the road clean in the moon.

He sat on the leather seat, the flies flaring constantly into the sweep of the headlamps, *worse than home* fading from his mind. He was driving with a priest in the night, his father and home miles away. This night he'd sleep in a strange house. He knew nothing.

The car slowed in the road of sycamores, and turned in open gates, the tyres sounding on the gravel. The church with its bell-rope dangling and the presbytery at the end of the circular drive were clear in the moon, the graveyard between, the headstones showing over the laurels along the drive. In the gravel clearing before the house the car stopped beside where a cactus flowered out of a bugled pedestal. He got out his case and coat and stood in the moon. Between the laurels of the drive a path of white gravel ran unbordered through the graves to the sacristy door.

"We have the good company of the dead about us," the priest smiled as if he'd read his mind, "but there's no need for them to disturb you, they do not walk, not till the Last Day."

"It's a strange feeling though."

"It'll pass, don't worry."

The house was cluttered with old and ponderous furniture, religious pictures in heavy gilt frames and an amazing collection of grandfather clocks on the walls. Two glasses with sandwiches and a jug of milk stood on a tray in the sitting-room.

"John has left us something. We might as well eat," the priest said and filled both glasses.

"Who is John?"

"I never told you, he keeps house for me."

"And is he old?"

"Younger than you, just sixteen. He's from a large family at the other end of the parish."

"Isn't it unusual for a boy?"

"I suppose. It was his mother mentioned to me that he was fond of housework, which is unusual, I suppose. I was driven crazy at the time with an old harridan of a priest's house-keeper who was trying at the time to run me and the parish as well as the house. So I suggested to the mother that he should come to me until he is eighteen, I'll try to use what influence I have to get him placed in a good hotel then. It's a career with enormous opportunity these days. So everyone is quite happy with the arrangement. I give him some train-ing, so I'd be glad while you're here if you're not free with him, treat him respectfully of course, but never forget that both of you are in unequal positions. Anything else would do his training no good."

They'd finished eating. The priest's eyes fixed on the mantelpiece where two delf bulldogs flanked a statue of St. Martin de Porres as he returned to his chair from leaving the tray back on the table.

"This is what I mean," he said. "He must have dusted the mantelpiece and look how he's arranged the things, absolutely no sense of placing."

He gazed respectfully as the priest changed the bulldogs to a position that satisfied him but he could see no difference now than before, just bulldogs about a statue of a small negro in brown and cream robes on the white marble.

"Absolutely no sense of taste, a very uncultivated people even after forty years of freedom the mass of Irish are. You just can't make silk out of sow's ear at the drop of a hat," he smiled and took off his Roman collar and lay back in the chair.

It was shocking to see a priest without his collar for the first time. The neck was chafed red. The priest looked human and frail.

"I always have to eat just before bed, since I was operated on, they cut two-thirds of my stomach away that time."

"When was that, father?"

"In Birmingham. I hadn't felt well for ages but put it on the long finger. Then I suddenly collapsed in the sacristy as I was unrobing myself after Mass. The surgeon said it was a miracle I pulled through."

He yawned and in the same sleepy movement began to unbutton his trousers. He drew up the shirt and vest to show his naked stomach, criss-crossed by two long scars, the blue toothmarks of the stitches clear. He showed the pattern of the operation with a finger spelling it out on the shocking white flesh.

"One-third has to do the work of the whole now, so it's why I have to eat late, you can never take much at any one sitting," he was saying as he replaced his clothes when a clock chimed once in the hallway. Its echoes hadn't died when another struck, harsher and more metallic, and then a medley of single strikes from all the house, startling when two clocks struck on the wall of the room.

"The last curate died here, he was a collector, and left them to the parish. They say the collection is worth something but you can't very well go and sell them so soon. They're a nuisance but John takes some curious delight in keeping them wound.

65

"It's one anyhow," he rose.

They knelt beside the armchairs, continual yawns impossible to suppress in the prayerful murmur.

Then he took the oil-lamp to show the way upstairs to the room.

12

"THERE'S THE WARDROBE, YOU CAN HANG YOUR CLOTHES. John's left a candle and matches. Would you like to light it before I go?"

"No, thanks, father, it's bright enough. I'll just get into bed."

"Don't worry about the morning. Sleep as long as you want. We'll call you for breakfast."

"What time will you say Mass, father?"

"Early but there's no need for you to go. You came a long journey. There'll be other mornings. If you're awake you'll hear noises."

"I'll probably be awake, father."

"If you are you can come down but it doesn't matter."

Yet he didn't move. He stayed with the lamp in his hand at the door, as if he expected to say a closer goodnight than the word, the collarless shirt was open on the chafed throat, and not the goodnight kiss your cursed father took years ago now on this priested mouth.

"Thanks, father. You're very good to me," you managed to shift away to the foot of the bed.

"I hope you sleep and are comfortable," he made uneasy pause before he dipped his fingers into the holy water container in the robes about the feet of the statue of the Virgin on the wall and sprinkled drops towards you and said, "Good night. God guard you."

"Good night, father," you said as you made the sign of the cross, and he was gone, the door closed.

You took the few things you'd brought out of the suitcase and left them in the wardrobe, the textbooks you hoped to study while you were here to one side on the bed, with the nightclothes. The moon came across the graveyard, its image cut in two by a diagonal crack in the dressing-table mirror the other end of the room. Underneath the window the car shone black on the gravel beside the cactus. Wild grasses twisted on the iron railings in the graveyard grew living and yellow. The bell-rope dangled from the tower down over the gravel path to the sacristy in the moonlight.

You had come. You were in the priest's house, you could draw back the linen sheet and get into bed. A picture of your father's house in your mind, all the others sleeping there miles away, and you here. Joan in bed in the town four miles away, all the world you knew mostly in bed in the night as you now too, Joan's voice, "It's even worse than home," in your ears, a moment passing, she must not be happy, you must find out more, you had no chance or you were too involved in your own affairs to make any effort, though what could be wrong.

Through the window the stones of the graveyard stood out beyond the laurels in the moon, all the dead about, lives as much filled with themselves and their importance once as you this night, indecision and trouble and yearning put down equal with laughing into that area of clay, and they lay calm as you would one eternal night while someone full of problems and uncertainties would lie as awake as you in a room.

At night they left their graves to walk in search of forgiveness, driven by remorse, you'd heard many times. They came most to the house of the priest to beg: the flesh same as their own and able to understand, but the unearthly power of God in his hands, power to pardon. But the house seemed still as the graveyard tonight.

The moment of death was the one real moment in life; everything took its proper position there, and was fixed for ever, whether to live in joy or hell for all eternity, or had your life been the haphazard flicker between nothingness and nothingness.

All pleasure was lost, whether you'd eaten flesh or worn roses, it was over, or whether you had gone bare and without. The wreaths and the Mass cards and the words meant nothing, these were for the living, to obscure the starkness with images of death, nothing got to do at all with the reality, just images of death for the living, images of life and love in black cloth.

The presence of the dead seemed all about, every stir of mouse or bird in the moonlit night, the crowded graves, the dead priest who'd collected the grandfather clocks. You grew frightened though you told yourself there was no reason for fear and still your fear increased, same in this bed as on the road in the country dark after people and cards, nothing about, till haunted by your own footsteps your feet go faster. You tell yourself that there's nothing to be afraid of, you stand and listen and silence mocks you, but you cannot walk calm any more. The darkness brushes about your face and throat. You stand breathing, but you can stand for ever for all the darkness cares. Openness is everywhere about you, and at last you take to your heels and run shamelessly, driven by the one urge to get to where there are walls and lamps.

In this room and house there was no place to run though,

only turn and turn, nothing but hooting silence and the hotness of your enfevered body when you held yourself rigid to
listen.

Real noises came. A door opened down the landing, it was
not shut. Feet padded on the boards, the whisper of clothes
brushing. You raised yourself on your hands, the grip of
terror close, for what could be moving at this hour of
night?

A low knock came on the door. Before you could say,
"Come in," it opened. A figure stood in the darkness along
the wall.

"You're not asleep?"

It was the priest's voice, some of the terror broke, you let
yourself back on your arms again.

"No," there was relief, but soon suspicion grew in place of
the terror, what could the priest want in the room at this
hour, the things that have to happen.

"I heard you restless. I couldn't sleep either, so I thought
it might be a good time for us to talk."

He wore a striped shirt and pyjamas, blue stripes on grey
flannel it seemed when he moved into the moonlight to draw
back a corner of the bedclothes.

"You don't mind, do you—it's easier to talk this way, and
even in the summer the middle of the night gets cold."

"No, father. I don't mind," what else was there to say, and
move far out to the other edge of the bed, even then his feet
touching you as they went down. The bodies lay side by side
in the single bed.

"You find it hard to sleep? I often do. It's the worst of all,
I often think, to be sleepless at night," he said, and you
stiffened when his arm went about your shoulder, was this to
be another of the midnight horrors with your father. His hand
closed on your arm. You wanted to curse or wrench yourself
free but you had to lie stiff as a board, stare straight ahead at

70

the wall, afraid before anything of meeting the eyes you knew were searching your face.

"Do you sleep well usually?"

"Alright, father. The first night in a strange house is hard."

"It's always hard in a strange house, if you're not a traveller. I used never be able to sleep the first night home from college, or the first night in the college after the holidays, what you're not used to I suppose, and the strange excitement."

His hand was moving on your shoulder. You could think of nothing to say. The roving fingers touched your throat. You couldn't do or say anything.

"You have a good idea why I invited you here?"

"Yes, father."

"I was going to broach it in the sitting-room, but I thought you might be too fagged out after the journey. When I heard you restless I thought it might be a good time to talk, in fact I thought it might be the cause of the restlessness. It's always better to talk no matter what. You've thought about the priesthood since? You know that that's one of the main reasons I wanted you here?"

"Yes, father."

"Have you come to any decision or any closer to one?" he moved his face closer to ask, his hand quiet, clasping tighter on the shoulder.

"No, father," you couldn't say any more, you had to fight back tears, it was too horrid and hopeless.

"You haven't decided either one way or the other?"

"No, father, but I don't know. I'm not sure."

You felt cornered and desperate, wanting to struggle far more free by this of the questions than the body and encircling arm.

"What troubles you most? Do you want to be a priest?"

"Yes, father."

"What then troubles you most?"

71

"I'm not sure if I have a vocation. I don't know."

"You know that God won't come down out of his heaven to call you. The Holy Father defined a vocation as three things: good moral character, at least average intelligence, a good state of health. If you have these and the desire to give your life to God, then you have a vocation, it's as easily recognizable as that. Does that help you to see your way any more clearly?"

"I don't think I'm good enough, father," was what you said twisting away from it put so close and plain as this, tears started to flow down your face.

"How?"

"I can't be certain. I thought maybe if I went out into the world for a few years to test myself, then I could be sure. It wouldn't be too late to become a priest then. Don't some become priests in that way?"

"It'd be unlikely. People get into ruts and habits and drift. Once you've got a taste of the world—it's hard to settle down at any time to the daily habitual service of God—but it's worse if you come late. It'd be unlikely you'd ever leave the world once you got its taste and if you did it would be harder than now. The excitement and novelty would soon go. And then and then and then."

He stopped, the conversation against a wall, and as suddenly his whole voice changed.

"Have you ever kissed a girl?" it came with the shock of a blow.

"No, father. Never."

"Have you ever wanted or desired to kiss?"

"Yes, father," the tears flowed hopelessly, just broken, he was cutting through to the nothingness and squalor of your life, you were now as you were born, as low as the dirt.

"Did you take pleasure in it?"

"Yes, father," it choked out.

72

"You excited yourself, brought them into your mind. You caused seed to spill in your excitement?"

"Yes, father."

"How often did it happen?"

"Several times a week sometimes. More times not at all."

"How many times a week?"

"Seven or eight sometimes, father."

"Did you try to break it?"

"Yes. Always after Confession."

"Did you succeed for long?"

"It's six weeks since it happened last."

"Did you bring one woman or many women into these pleasures?"

"Many women, father."

"Were they real or imaginary?"

"Both, father."

"You don't think this vice has got a grip on you, you think you could break it?"

"Yes, father, I think I might."

"This is the most reason why you're not sure, why you think you're not good enough, is it?"

"Yes, father. Do you think I might be good enough?"

You still felt a nothing and broken, cheap as dirt, but hope was rising, would the priest restore the wreckage, would he say—yes, yes, you're good enough.

"I don't see any reason why not if you fight that sin."

Joy rose, the world was beautiful again, all was beautiful.

"Had you ever to fight that sin when you were my age, father?" you asked, everything was open, you could share your lives, both of you fellow-passengers in the same rocked boat.

There was such silence that you winced, you had committed an impertinence, you were by no means in the same boat, you were out there alone with your sins.

"The only thing I see wrong with you is that you take things far too serious, and bottle them up, and brood," he completely ignored the question. "Most of those in my youth who became priests were gay. They kicked football, they went to dances in the holidays, flirted with girls, even sometimes saw them home from the dances. They made good normal priests."

You barely listened this time, resentment risen close to hatred. He had broken down your life to the dirt, he'd reduced you to that, and no flesh was superior to other flesh. You'd wanted to share, rise on admittance together into joy, but he was different, he was above that, you were impertinent to ask. He must have committed sins the same as yours once too, if he was flesh.

What right had he to come and lie with you in bed, his body hot against yours, his arm about your shoulders. Almost as the cursed nights when your father used stroke your thighs. You remembered the blue scars on the stomach by your side.

"You must pray to God to give you Grace to avoid this sin, and be constantly on your guard. As you grow older you'll find your passion easier to control. It weakens," he was saying. "You can stay here long as you want, you'll have time and quiet to think, you can bring any trouble or scruple to me. We can talk. And pray, as I will pray for you too, that God may well direct you."

He paused. You'd listened with increasing irritation and hatred, you wished the night could happen again. You'd tell him nothing. You'd give him his own steel.

You felt him release his arm and get out on the floor and replace the bedclothes. Your hands clenched as he sprinkled holy water on your burning face, though the drops fell cool as sprigs of parsley.

"God guard you and bless you. Sleep if you can," he said as he left the room noiselessly as he'd entered it.

13

ANGUISH STAYED AFTER THE PRIEST HAD GONE—RAGE, YOU'D
been stripped down to the last squalor, and no one had right
to do that to anybody: shame, what must the priest think of you
every time he looked at you any more: and if it could happen
again what you'd say and not say, what you'd want to happen,
you'd give nothing away, you'd destroy him, but it was all
over now, except for the feverish restlessness of the anguish.
The moonlight was still in the room, the crack across the
mirror. The clocks beat the half-hours, single quick chimes,
but you couldn't tell the hours, none of the clocks struck
alone or together, just one broken medley. And it was impossible to sleep, the mind a preying whirl.

At last, restless and hot, you reached out and found a sock
across your shoes on the floor, pulled your prick till it grew
stiff, and you could push it into the sock. You were all dis-

turbed and it was something to do and it would draw off some of the fever. You turned and started to pump, rhythmically but without imagination till you heard the springs creaking. You moved out to the very edge of the bed, where the solid rail was under the mattress. You imagined nothing, neither edge of nylon nor pink nipple in your teeth, nor hands thrusting through your hair, but just pumped mechanical as a slow piston up and down, you got hot and you could press your mouth on the pillow, pumping madly, till you started to beat out into the sock. You turned at the last flutter, so that it wouldn't have chance to seep through the wool and stain the sheet. Wet came on your hand as you removed the sock and let it fall over the shoes on the floor again. You were able to lie on your back and stare at the ceiling in more stupor than calm.

You'd broken the three weeks discipline since Confession, you'd not be able to go to Communion in the morning. You'd never be able to be a priest either, you'd drift on without being able to decide anything, it was easier to let it go. You shivered as the interrogation of an hour ago came back, the squalor, but it was better try and shut it out.

The clocks kept up their insane medley, the single strikes of the half-hours, the medley of the hours. The yellow of the moonlight faded as the day grew light. You stared at the ceiling, different number of boards than over the old bed with the broken brass bells at home, so much variation too in the grain and the knots.

"Will the morning ever come, ever come, ever come?" as you waited for the cursed clocks, until you could stand it no longer, and dressed and went down outside, holding the knocker as you closed the hall door so as to make no noise.

The white ground mist filled the morning, promise of a blazing day, the church vague in white twenty yards away. A spider netting of it lay on the laurels, on the cactus leaves

76

above the iron bugle, it lay on the grass across the graves. Your hand left a gleaming black handtrack on the mudguard of the car, your feet left shining wet tracks on the grass between the graves.

Your cheeks burned with the fever of fatigue, you wished you could lie naked on all this wet coolness and suck and roll your face in the wet grass, press the hot pores of your body against the wetness.

You noticed nothing except these and the flitting of a wren low in the laurels. You ground your teeth, your hands clenched and unclenched, the mind bent on destruction of the night before, but only managing to circle and circle in its own futility.

You couldn't be a priest, never now, that was all. You'd never raise anointed hands. You'd drift into the world, world of girls and women, company in gay evenings, exact opposite of the lonely dedication of the priesthood unto death. Your life seemed set, without knowing why, it was fixed, you had no choice. You were a drifter, you'd drift a whole life long after pleasure, but at the end there'd be the reckoning. If you could be a priest you'd be able to enter that choking moment without fear, you'd have already died to longing, you'd have already abandoned the world for that reality, there'd be no confusion. But the night and room and your father and even the hedge around the orchard at home were all confusion, there was no beginning nor end.

In the grappling the things of the morning lost their starkness, you were standing lost between the graves when the door opened, and the priest was there, in his soutane, a jug and heavy latchkey in his hand.

"Good morning. I didn't expect to find you afoot so early."

"Good morning, father. I couldn't sleep much."

"The first night in a strange house is always bad. By the look of the mist the day'll be another scorcher."

77

'It looks as if it's going to be hot, father. It's nearly always hot when the mist's like that," the pingball went, and did you wonder how much of your life would go on these courteous noises.

"Would you like to serve Mass for me?" the priest said, you'd joined each other on the gravel path.

"I'd be glad to, father."

"Usually John serves it, but a break will do him no harm. He'll have breakfast for us soon as it's over."

"That's fine so, father."

"We're not very likely to have worshippers. No one comes on the weekdays except seldom. It's the real country."

With the latchkey he unlocked the sacristy door, then went out through the altar and down to the main door, where he lifted off the heavy iron bar, and opened both doors wide. The cruets had to be filled with water and wine, the bowl with water, the white cloth laid across. He gave you a soutane and surplice of his own to wear.

"We're ready now, but it's not eight yet," he said when they stood robed before the crucifix on the sacristy wall. "A Miss Brady, a retired schoolmistress, used come but she hasn't put in an appearance for over a week, I think she may be gone to the sea, but we'd better wait till eight just in case."

There was silence in the sacristy, except for birds outside, waiting for eight, now as always tension of something strange about to happen, and then both of you bowing together to the crucifix at eight.

You had to concentrate too much to wander or think during the Mass, follow the words and movements to make the responses, pour wine and water, ring the small bell though no one was there to hear, and change the missal. The priest moved as in a dream, in the formality of the ritual and black vestments of the dead, nothing whatever to the priest of the night before.

78

You served too the rite as in a dream, the bread and wine were utterly changed without you knowing. Only at the Communion did any disturbance come, you could not receive, you had sinned. You watched the priest but he didn't seem to notice or else it meant nothing to him. Then dumbly you went and poured the last water and wine and followed the Mass through to its end.

Breakfast was ready in the house. A boy of fifteen with blond hair, his face so pale that it seemed to belong more to the city than here, came with the tea, and the priest said, "John, this is Mr. Mahoney."

"You're welcome here, sir," the boy smiled as he shook your hand, and you could get nothing out, you'd never been called Mr. Mahoney or sirred before, it was too unreal.

The newspaper had come. The priest commented on the headlines, and then as he folded it up towards the end of breakfast he said, "They're such a waste of time, but strange the grip they get on you, it's habit or curiosity, you feel there's something important that you may miss. It's some sort of illusion that you're in contact with a greater world outside your own little corner."

"I suppose so, father. I never thought of it like that."

It went so, nothing was spoken of the night before. The priest said he had to go away for the day. He'd not be back till the late evening.

"You can amuse yourself in any way you wish. John will get you your lunch. There are books, the key's in the bookcase, you can search and find for yourself. I used to spend a lot of my holidays with Uncle Michael, the Canon now, and I used read and read.

"You know you can stay as long as you wish: a week, or a fortnight. I'll be away a good deal. You'll have plenty of time to think and come to a decision. You can make yourself completely free and at home."

79

"Thank you, father," you bowed your head, there was nothing else to say.

The priest went and gave some instructions to John, then he left, offering no explanation for his going, nor could you ask. You watched the car turn round the pedestal, the tyres crunching on the gravel, and you answered the priest's wave before he went out of sight on the circling drive of laurel and through the gates that no one seemed to ever close.

14

ONCE BACK IN THE ROOM YOU HAD THE PURE DAY ON YOUR
hands, without distraction, except what you wished to be
without, the fears and doubts and longings, coming and going.

The mahogany bookcase stood solid. Scott, Dickens, Canon
Sheehan under glass: Wordsworth, Milton, volumes in brown
leather, gold on the spines: staunch religious books, doctrine,
histories of the church, books of sermons. One lone paper-
back, Tolstoy's *Resurrection* in a red and white Penguin, and
you turned the small key to get it out, though you'd never
heard of it or Tolstoy. It didn't look such a tomb as the
others, there were more green leaves and living light of the
day about it than the dust and memory of the others, it
was too new for many dead hands to have turned the
pages.

You took it outside, your feet on the ground. The sun was beating through the last shades of mist, the blazing day close. You watched the cactus, colour of ripe vegetable marrow, and wondered had it religious significance, the one place you'd seen it before was in front of the Convent of Mercy in Longford, in a bugled pedestal too, and surrounded too by white gravel, but that faded, to look at the yellow cactus long enough was to come to silence and fear.

But where were you to go? What were you to do with yourself and this book?

Round by the side was the apple garden. The white paint was new on the iron gate. Just inside was a green seat, fuchsia bushes overhanging it, their bells so brute red, and the purple tongues. You sat there, and looked at the row of cabbages beyond the apple trees, and then turned to the book, but not for long.

Why are you here? the questioning started.

To sit and read a book.

But no, beyond that, why did you come, why are you alone here?

To think about being a priest.

You'll not be able. Even last night you had to sin again. You weren't able to go to Communion this morning. The only reason you stopped abuse for the last weeks was to be able to put a face on it before the priest.

You want to go out into the world? You want girls and women, to touch their dresses, to kiss, to hold soft flesh, to be held in their caressing arms? To bury everything in one swoon into their savage darkness?

Dream of peace and loveliness, charm of security: picture of one woman, the sound of *wife*, a house with a garden and trees near the bend of a river. She your love waiting at a wooden gate in the evening, her black hair brushed high, a mustard-coloured dress of corduroy or whipcord low from the throat, a boy and a girl, the girl with a blue ribbon in her hair, playing on the grass. You'd lift and kiss them, girl and boy. Then softly kiss her, your wife and love, secrets in eyes. Picnics down the river Sunday afternoons, playing and laughing on the river-bank, a white cloth spread on the grass. Winter evenings with slippers and a book, in the firelight she is playing the piano. In the mirror you'd watch her comb her black hair, so long, the even brush strokes. The long nights together, making love so gently it lingered for hours, your lips kissing, "I love you. I love you, my darling. I am so happy." A Christmas of rejoicing and feasting. You'd hear the thawing snow outside slip from the branches, the radio playing:

> *I'm dreaming of a white Christmas,*
> *Just like the ones I used to know.*

World of happiness without end.

You'd have to give that up to be a priest, but it would come to nothing on its own anyhow, the moments couldn't be for long escaped. Death would come. Everything riveted into that. Possession of neither a world nor a woman mattered then, whether you could go to the Judgment or not without flinching was all that would matter. I strove as fierce as I was able, would be a lot to be able to say. A priest could say that. He'd chosen God before life.

Though who wanted happiness of heaven, to sing hymns for ever in an eternal garden, no change and no hunger or longing.

Hell was there too, the fires and crawling worms, sweat and curses, the despair of for ever. How would the innocent afternoons on the river look from hell, the brush strokes through the black hair in the mirror. Was it better never to know happiness so that there'd be no anguish of loss. A priest could have no anguish, he'd given up happiness, his fixed life moving in the calm of certainty into its end, cursed by no earthly love or longing, all had been chosen years before.

Yet your father was no priest, he'd gone out into the world, played football in the Rock Field, danced in the summer marquees and at winter parties under the mistletoe: he'd married, children had come, and he didn't seem to have got much sweetness. But what has your father's life got to do with your life?

If you married you would plant a tree to deny and break finally your father's power, completely supplant it by the graciousness and marvel of your life, but as a priest you'd remain just fruit of the cursed house gone to God.

If you became a priest, would you not be crazed on your deathbed because of the way you'd cheated your life out of human fulfilment, never to have loved and received love, never to have married in the June of passion. Three months of it would have been a great gift.

I married when I was passionately in love, would be something to look back on no matter what the present horror. It would be something too to haunt you, you'd always hanker after it, it was the red rose of life, you'd never been even given it for a day.

Though what was the use, there was no escape. You were only a drifter and you'd drift. You couldn't carry the responsibility of a decision. You were only a hankerer. You'd drift and drift. You'd just dream of the ecstasy of destruction on a woman's mouth.

You were sitting on a green bench in the morning, was that not enough. The sun was blazing clear as glass. Your hands were damp with sweat. A ceaseless hum was droning into the heat. You could take off your coat and tie.

Six apple trees stood in the garden: three cookers, a honeycomb, Beauty of Bath, apples with the rust of pears and not ripe till the frosts. Jam-jars half full of syrup hung on twine from the branches. Wasps circled and circled the rims before they were tempted into the struggling froth of the dead and dying trapped in the sweetness. Some apples had fallen on the ground, shells of flaming colour, rotting brown of the flesh eaten far as the skins. The Beauty of Baths on the tree were cold and sharp, the teeth shivered once they sank in, there was nothing to do but throw it out of sight into the tall cocksfoot along the hedge.

You left coat and tie with the Penguin on the seat and idled back into the graveyard, alive with bees moving between the small flowers of the graves. There was such heat and nothingness now. A white clover at your feet swayed under the clambering of a sucking bee. You watched it, the trembling flower, the black bee unsteady and awkward on the ruffled whiteness, and suddenly you jumped and trampled bee and flower into the earth of the grave. More were moving between the red and white and yellow heads in the sunshine. You could turn it into a sport, tramp bee after bee down, it'd amuse the morning, you could keep a count, as they grew scarce in the graveyard the stalking'd grow more difficult. Nero used tear wings off flies above Rome once, though what was the use. After all you were in the graveyard in the day.

This place was such a green prison. The wall of sycamores shut it away from the road. The tall graveyard hedges and the steep furze-covered hill at the back of the house, only one green patch in its centre where a lone donkey grazed, closed it to the fields around, it ran to no horizon. There was little movement. A general noise of machinery came. A car or van went by behind the sycamore screen. Two living voices in conversation drifted from some field. Somewhere a hen cackled with fright. Here was only interest of the graves and names, the verses, the dates, the weeds and withered wreaths, the ghastly artificial roses and lilies under globes of glass. You could make a catalogue of all these, they'd pass the time just

85

as well as the slaughter of bees, whatever either would really do. The day would probably go its own way anyhow.

The toll of a funeral bell sounded close, after a minute a slow second followed. What was obviously a funeral went past through the sycamores, shod hooves coming clean through the noise of motors. John came towards you out of the house.

"I was wondering where the bell is ringing from, John."

"From the Protestant church, sir. Mr. Munro's funeral is there today, sir."

It brought you to a halt, the sirring was so strange, you'd never been sirred by anyone before, and there seemed no reason for it now either. It was as uncomfortable as any pretending.

"Why do you call me *sir*, John? We're not much different in years or anything."

He stopped. A quick flash showed in the eyes, and the pale face flushed.

"I don't know, sir. You're stopping here, sir," he said doggedly, after a long embarrassed pause, a dogged defiance in the voice, you'd blundered, though you'd never discover how from him. The slow tolling of the Protestant bell continued.

"Have you to go far?" you tried to make conversation on the gravel.

"Just to the church to ring the Angelus, sir. It's probably better to wait till the funeral's over now, sir."

"Are there many Protestants here?"

"About half as many as Catholics but they have the good land, sir."

At the church door he caught the wire bell-rope in his hand but he didn't pull it till he was sure the last funeral toll had sounded. You blessed yourself and tried to pray but couldn't, his white arms went up and down with the bell-rope, that was all.

86

"What time would you like your lunch at, sir?" he asked when he'd finished.

"I'm not particular, whatever time is easy for you."

"In about an hour so, sir. At one."

"That'll be all right, if it's easy for you then."

"Thanks, sir."

You watched him on the gravel to the front door. The sirring was strange, the boy housekeeper, you here alone in the day, it was all baffling and strange.

What was there to do for the hour but wander, from gravel to grave to garden, examine the cactus leaves, wonder what your father was doing at this time, shudder at the memory of the night before, the mind not able to stay on anything for long. When the hands touched anything they wanted to grip it tight enough for the knuckles to whiten and the hour went hours long, real relief when the absurd gong was struck at exactly one for lunch.

You'd no hunger but you forced yourself to eat. There was too much clamminess even with the doors and windows open. From time to time you had to lay down the knife and fork to crush a sucking leg. John came and went but would not be drawn into conversation.

Afterwards you stood in front of the mantelpiece of white marble with its bulldogs and St. Martin de Porres before you tried the bookcase again. You took out several books and it was the same performance each time. Your eye roved angrily over the print, you replaced it and took out another, replaced it, on and on, till you hurled a big history on the floor, and jumped on it with rage, crying, "I'll do for you, I'll do for you, do for you."

The fit brought release once it spent itself. You wondered if John had heard in the kitchen, you must be half going crazy. You wondered if the damage to the book on the floor would ever be noticed. Then you picked it up and with sense of foolishness replaced it in the press and turned the key. You sat again in the chairs. The collection of clocks started up the confused medley of another half-hour.

This utter sense of decrepitude and dust over the house—the clocks, the bulldogs, the mahogany case of books, the black leather armchairs, the unlived in room. At least in your own house there was life, no matter what little else.

In these houses priests lived, you'd be alone in one of them one day too, idling through the pages of books, reading the Office as you walked between the laurels. Girls in summer dresses would stroll past free under the sycamores. You could go to the sick rooms to comfort the defeated and the dying. People would come to the door to have Masses said for their wishes and their dead, they'd need certificates of birth and marriage, letters of freedom. It was summer now. It'd be hardly different with newspapers and whiskey watching the pain of the leaves fall and the rain gather to drip the long evenings from the eaves.

Though that was far ahead, it didn't remove your presence from this actual day, in this black leather armchair, a vision of green laurels through the window. The best thing was to go somewhere.

"No. It's worse than home," Joan had said the night before, it was impossible to know what was wrong, you'd not remembered it much either, too squalidly involved in your own affairs. It brought new lease of energy, at least that much. It'd be better to tell John before going. He was in his shirt-sleeves, baking, when you went down, the smell of stewing apples mixed with the dough.

"I'm sorry," you had to apologize when he started. "I wondered is the town far?"

"Three miles or about, sir."

"You could walk it in an hour?"

"Yes. Easy, sir."

88

"I think I'll go so—to see my sister. Did you see her since she came?"

"She was out two Sundays, sir," he said everything guardedly, there was no use.

"Will you tell Father where I've gone if he comes before me?"

You looked at John, you wished you could talk, whether he was happy here or not, how long more he'd stay with the priest and where he'd go then, if he had interest in books or sports or anything, but you couldn't, and the more you heard of the sirring the more unreal it got.

"Good-bye so, John."

"Good-bye so, sir."

Across the stone stile out by the front of the church you went into the cool of the sycamores, a few hundred yards down the road the Protestant church where the funeral bell had tolled. The sycamores gave way there, and the narrow dirt-track ran between high grass margins with thorn hedges out of which ash saplings rose. You had to carry your coat on your arm the day was so hot. Close to the town tar replaced the earth and stones, the day full of the smell of melting tar, sticking to your shoes to gather the dust and fine pebbles. The gnawing in the guts started as you came into the town and kept on towards Ryan's.

15

RYAN WAS SELLING SANDALS TO A CUSTOMER, AND NO SIGN OF Joan in the shop. He smiled recognition, the teeth more than the servility of the eyes said he was sorry to be engaged, he'd be finished in a minute, he'd consider it a great favour if you could possibly wait.

Eventually the sale was completed. He rattled out assurances as he covered the box with brown paper and tied it with twine. With fawning gratitude and wishes of good luck he saw the woman far as the door.

"A pleasant surprise to see you," he shook hands with you smiling. "I'm sorry to have kept you waiting. It's such bad weather for business, everyone making too much use of the sunshine, and hard to blame them to come to the shops. You get fed up waiting and fixing the shelves. But the rain, the rain will come, and it'll be different."

"I hope it's alright to come," you said when the flood subsided.

"Perfectly alright. You come to see Joan, isn't it? It's perfectly alright."

"Father Malone is away. So I thought I'd come in to see Joan for an hour."

"Perfectly alright, she'll be delighted. She's in the kitchen."

He led the way in through the counter, and opened the kitchen door to let you in the first. Joan was scrubbing at the sink, and she looked up startled.

"I have a pleasant surprise for you, Joan. Your brother has come to take you out on the town. So run and change."

"But I'm almost finished," she reddened.

"It doesn't matter, it'll wait for again. You better make use of the sunshine while it lasts."

She went sideways to the stairs, drying her hands as she went in the apron, smiling in servile gratitude or apology. You were glad when she went, you took the idiotic formal smile of pleasantness off your own face, and turned to Ryan who stood at the open door to the shop. He offered a cigarette and joked, "No bad habits I see," when it was refused, and he was lighting his own.

Through the big window your eyes went out to the garden and you started. The two daughters of the night before were lobbing a tennis ball over and back across a loosely strung net, wearing swimsuits and ornate white sandals instead of usual tennis dress. Their mother sat in the shade of plum trees along the back wall, a newspaper spread across her lap in the deck-chair, and she was too far away to know whether she was dozing or following the casual play.

"Two fine lazy pieces," Ryan said, he'd followed your eyes through the window. "Someone else will wear himself to the

91

bone to keep them before long. They have the right ideas already. They can't get enough of dances. You're very quiet, I hear? You don't go to the dances?"

"No. I don't go to the dances," and already resentment had started.

White wool of a new tennis ball hung in the air and a racket swung. Arm and straining thigh flashed in the stroke, the body stiffening sheer nakedly in the apple-green swimsuit, and you had to pull your eyes away in fear.

"Tempting?" Ryan smiled, and rage rushed again. You wanted to smash Ryan's face in, to defile and slash the stripped girls in the garden, to kick into the trunks of thighs that opened under the newspaper in the deck-chair. But all you could do was clench hands and wait till Joan came. You managed to answer his, "Have a nice time," politely enough too as you left.

You weren't very far down the street though when you burst out violently, "You were scrubbing clothes and they were in the garden. And he asked me in the kitchen if I found his cursed daughters tempting. He asked me if I thought they were tempting."

"That'd be true enough to form," she said uneasily, it brought some quiet, it made you feel selfishly involved with your own affairs again.

"You said it was worse than home?"

"Yes," she was uncertain.

"In what way?"

"She makes you feel bad about everything and I'm afraid of him."

"How?"

"The first day," and she was breaking, "I was on a stool putting shoe-boxes up on the shelves and he put his hands right up my dress and that was only the beginning. Once he got me in the bathroom and it was horrible. I'm always afraid. And then he takes it out on you in other ways," and she began to cry violently.

"No, you mustn't cry, not in the street, wait, Joan, we'll soon be out of the town."

That much had to be slowly dragged, and when it came it was too much, it would be better to have waited, but how your hands hungered for their throats. They could sit on deck-chairs under the plum trees and look at tennis, naked but for the swimsuits. Why couldn't Ryan climb on his wife in the deck-chair, that's what he had married her for, or couldn't he tear off the swimsuits and straddle the pampered daughters or be whipped naked down the streets. And if you could get him into that bathroom for one minute you'd choke him.

Across the stone bridge at the foot of the town the feet went, out to bungalows with port-holes one side of the front door, and the effort or rhythm of the walking brought some calm. You didn't want to hear anything more but to get her away.

"How much money have you, Joan?"

"A pound and two shillings. I bought these sandals and the dress and you can't save much out of ten shillings," she was apologizing about the sandals and the dress she wore, that you hadn't even noticed.

"No. I just wanted to know. I had enough to get both of us home tomorrow but we have plenty now."

"To go home tomorrow?"

"Yes—both of us. You couldn't stay on in that hole?"

"But what'll he say?"

"Our father?"

"Yes."

"He'll say nothing. We'll tell him what happened, that you couldn't stay on, that's all. It doesn't matter much what he says."

"Who'll tell them in the shop?"

"I will, if you want, unless you'd sooner do it yourself."

"No. You'll tell. I'm afraid. Do you think will everything be alright?"

"It'll be alright."

The grass margin a short way beyond the last of the houses was an easy place to rest, and not many people or cars passed.

"Does Father Gerald know you're going tomorrow?"

"No. I'll tell him when I get back."

"I thought you were staying more than a week?"

"I'm not now. I'm going tomorrow."

"Are you not going to be a priest?"

"I don't know, I don't think so. What made you think I was ever going to be a priest anyhow?"

"You were always very quiet or something," and that caused you to start, you didn't think yourself very quiet.

You didn't know very much about yourself so. The mirror was before you now, temptation to probe to see other pictures of you in her mind, but it was no use, she had her life as well as you, every life had too much importance and unimportance to be only a walking mirror for another.

You walked slowly back past the bungalows and then the shops. Ryan was behind the counter.

"So you got back, did you," he greeted. "Mrs. Ryan is inside. I think she expects you to stay to tea. Come on inside anyhow."

Inside she was laying the table for tea.

"I was cross when I heard you came and I wasn't told. You'll stay to tea. The children said too they'd like very much for you to stay," she invited.

"I'm sorry. I left word that I'd be back for tea and Father Malone may be waiting for me. But thank you very much."

"That seems a shame . . ." she was beginning.

"I just want to tell you that Joan is coming home with me tomorrow," you had to grow tense to force it out, but you remembered the bathroom.

Her eyes searched for her husband's, but they told her nothing, except to deal with the situation herself, she was the dominant one.

"That's a bit of a surprise."

"I'm sorry."

"People usually give more notice than that."

"I'm sorry but she has to come with me tomorrow."

"You're being very sorry but what has she to say for herself?"

"What I say," and you felt your control of yourself slip, you had to cut it short before you were driven to attack. "I'm sorry. I must go. Be ready tomorrow, I'll call for you before the bus time."

She stood without any attempt to make response. The woman had grown swollen with suppressed anger. You didn't know whether you said good-bye again or sorry before you left, you were too anxious to be gone, before your control slipped.

You went the same road back, rage seething, and failure. People had to go among people, they needed other people, yet they couldn't be easy, all the little hatchets that came up. Wouldn't it be better for them to stay alone in the fields and rooms, and let the world come or pass in whatever shape it would? Why couldn't the Ryans listen to you tell them that Joan was leaving and no more, instead of driving knives at you, and why had you the same urge to knife them back? Then you couldn't think when you imagined that meek bastard alone with her in the bathroom.

All the strength, the will to go on, was drained by the quarrel and what she'd said, nothing but anger and dust and despair, always the same after all these useless conflicts with your father or here. You felt close to the end, feverish and worn, the day's sun dying above you into the west, and then you tried to walk quicker, watching your shoes swing over the road, how so much dust had dulled their shine since you had left.

16

THE CAR WAS ONE SIDE OF THE CACTUS, THE PRIEST SITTING IN
one of the black leather armchairs in the room with a newspaper. He would not look up. He turned each page with as
much crackle as he could. He was annoyed, and what did you
care, you wished you could go away out of his annoyance,
leave him there, you'd enough turmoil and conflict for one
day.

"Did you eat yet?" he consented to ask at last out of the
newspaper, you weren't in the room to him till then though
you'd been standing stupidly for five minutes inside the door.

"No, father."

"Then we'd better have it so now. I delayed mine."

He rose, folded the newspaper and let it fall back in the
chair, and he went out and struck the gong in the hall. You
followed him out to where the table was laid in the dining-
room. Almost immediately John came with the soup.

"I more or less understood you were to stay about the house today," he brought out his grievance as he sprinkled salt and pepper on his soup.

"Yes, but I wanted to see Joan. I didn't think it would be any harm."

"Were you not interfering with her work? If your day was free hers wasn't. Could you not have waited for the two of us to go in together to see her?"

He was using the same pressure of the night before. He was the one who decided—or was he. He'd not have his own way so easy this evening. You didn't answer.

"And what did you do in town?" he had to ask.

"Mr. Ryan gave her time off. We went out the town for a walk."

This evening would not be his as last night was.

"She's coming home with me tomorrow."

"She's coming home with you tomorrow," he lifted his face, puzzled and ironic emphasis on every word.

"She wasn't happy there. She wants to come with me tomorrow."

"This news is quite sudden I must say. How is she not happy?"

"They interfered with her."

"Who?"

"Ryan did."

"How did he interfere?"

"Sexually."

"You have proof of this?"

"No, but she told me. She'd hardly want to tell lies."

"How did she say he was interfering?"

"He attacked her in the bathroom once. There were several other things."

"Why didn't this come out before?"

"She was frightened. She was afraid to tell."

98

"Did you attack the Ryans with this?"

"No. I told them she was leaving with me tomorrow. I gave no reasons."

"For that relief much thanks at least."

John came with the main course. He took away the empty soup bowls. There was silence while the priest portioned the food out of the dish.

"You've decided to go home tomorrow?"

"Yes, father."

"You've more or less made up your mind about your life so?"

You'd never make up your mind but it was simpler to pretend you had.

"I don't think I'm able for to be a priest, father."

Another slow interval of silence, sharp noises of knives or forks on the plate, a thrush or something singing beyond the open window out in the graveyard.

"May God bless your life no matter what its way is all that's left to me to say so," he said, and nothing had prepared you for it, he went on, he spoke very slow: "I was afraid today that maybe I had pressed you too hard last night. There never was such need of priests in the world. But no priest at all is better than a bad priest. You may not be able to save your soul as a priest. There are far greater stresses, greater responsibility, greater temptations than in the ordinary or natural way of life. You stand on a height. And heights were never safe places for humans. You can fall, you can make worry over your health or car fill the place of a wife and children. Did you ever hear of the word *bourgeoisie*?"

"Yes, father. I did."

"It comes out of French strangely enough. Most of us in Ireland will soon be that, fear of the poor-house is gone, even the life your father brought you up on won't last hardly twenty years more. A priest who ministers to the *bourgeoisie* becomes more a builder of churches, bigger and more comfortable churches, and schools than a preacher of the Word of God. The Society influences the Word far more than the Word influences the Society. If you are a good priest you have to walk a dangerous plank between committees on one hand and Truth or Justice on the other. I often don't know. I often don't know."

He paused on some futility or despair.

"There's a notion that once you've taken your ordination vows that there's no more trouble. People have the same charming illusion about marriage too. They'll stay happily married by saying a few words one morning at an altar, but everything has to be struggled for. A priest has to do it utterly alone, alone with his life and his God, there are not any dramas of quarrel and reunion about that. It's not easy, day after day."

His words, so different to anything he'd ever shown you in his life before, changed the day by magic, though you didn't fully understand what he said. It became one call to struggle and sacrifice.

"I thought I might be a priest after a few years, when I'd be more certain," they moved you to say.

"It's unlikely," he brought that to a halt. "I'm not so sure of late vocations. Life is very short. There's something not nice about making a gift of worn clothes. You can do good in any way of life, a person is always more important than any way. If a man chooses a way of life he should try and stick to it. Changing doesn't matter. You'll have yourself on your hands at the end of all change.

"Would you care to walk outside? That's if you're not tired after the town. It's very fine, the evening," the priest's voice was restless and excited.

"No. I'm not tired. I'd like to, father."

The evening gave no shock of cold, it was so close and warm, midges were beginning to swarm.

Shoes crunched on the gravel as you walked between the laurels, from the car at the cactus to the bell-rope dangling before the church door, the first fading traces of the light, the moon a pale vapour above. On the gravel the shoes went back and forward.

"Don't throw things in the ditch no matter what happens. You'll be tempted. Your faith will weaken. Doubt will grow like cancer. You'll be rebuked by other people doing better in the world than you, but do not mind. Remember your life is a great mystery in Christ and that nothing but your state of mind can change. And pray. It's not merely repetition of words. It's a simple silent act of turning the mind on God, the contemplation of the mystery, the Son of God going by way of Palm Sunday to Calvary and on to Easter."

"Yes, father," you answered, somewhere you'd felt or known that before though you couldn't say how or when.

"Though remember I'd do Peter on this in public before I'd admit it. They'd think they'd a madman for curate, and that'd do no one good. I'd deny it in public. It'd only cause trouble for me and everyone."

You'd never heard talk of this kind before. Everything seemed to grow more complicated.

"Thank you, father," you said, mechanical.

"For what?" he reacted sharply.

"For telling me," you fumbled, out of depth.

"No, don't thank me. Someone told me much the same once, it doesn't matter much who. The man's dead. But it was one thing I never lost, it meant something. I've told you now. The debt is paid back in some way. It is a great mystery.

"Don't think I'm a saint because I'm a priest and know things hundreds knew. I'd probably deny it before a crowd, to myself even on another night. I have some reason to believe that even the most stupid and mean are visited many times by consciousness of the mystery. You see it especially after the feasts of food and wine, around Christmas, in the dregs of a wedding day. That it's safely killed doesn't matter. We all want to enjoy ourselves in eternal day. Security, that's what everyone's after, security."

What he said didn't matter. He'd moved deeps within you that you could not follow. He was so changed: was this the same man that had showed you scars on his belly, the arm and voice of the night before, he who'd been resentful of you over the meal because you'd left the house to see Joan. Yet it must be. It must be that something had broken, a total generosity flowing.

"You can do me one favour."

"What, father?"

"Remember me in your prayers, as I'll remember you."

"I will, father."

"The midges, not even my cigarette smoke keeps them away, a sign of rain they say," he was anxious to change.

"My father says that too."

"Strange how uneasy people get when they've really spoken," his own pace had quickened. "All the things we say. And how little of all the words even touch any reality. Or perhaps they all do if we knew it," he changed to laugh lightly.

"None of what I said was meant to make you uneasy. Only because I was uneasy myself. I'm not usually like this, hardly ever, I don't know what got into me," his hand rested a split second on your shoulder in reassurance.

The summer night was there, the sense of damp or dew. The moon was pale but out, the smoke of rain about it. The shadows stretched lightly on the gravel. Sense of dusk was about the grass and growths of the graves, about the pale shining laurels. The pores of the cactus must be open to the cool and dampness.

"Perhaps we'd better go in. John may have something for us."

Biscuits and glasses of cold milk waited inside on the table. The clocks chimed. The priest said he had to do some private things: you were free to stay up or go to bed. Tiredness and the burden of nothing to do drove you to bed. You fell immediately asleep.

It was late when you woke, past ten on the clocks downstairs.

Father Gerald had already said Mass. John had served.

"I looked in at eight but you were sleeping. I didn't want to wake you. You have the long journey before you today," he said.

That you were going home today was a shock. With Joan, before evening, you'd face your father. Now that it was lost, this house with the priest and John seemed a world where you could have stayed. You wished you could tell Father Gerald that you wanted to stay here for the rest of the holidays. You wished you could tell him that you were on your way to be a priest. You'd stay here in the long summers from Maynooth. But that was changed, it was lost, and there was a horror of attraction about it now that it was lost, your dream had strayed about it now, and you felt the pain as you poured milk over the cornflakes and tried to eat.

The windows were bleared with a soft steady drizzle outside and after breakfast you sat with the priest and read newspapers and watched out on the laurels shining with wet and the fresh dark gravel and the wet roof of the church.

He drove you into town when it was time, almost far as Ryan's door but not quite.

"You're on your own now," he said. "There's going to be no pleasantness over Joan's going like this and I can't seem to get involved. I have to remain in the parish. I'm their priest."

"It's alright, father. I didn't expect you. You were very kind to drive me in. Thank you, father."

"Good-bye. God guard you."

You watched the car away, the tyres swishing in the wet. A sickness rose as you faced for Ryan's, what was the use of all this effort, you wanted not to have to.

"I wonder if you could tell her I'm here, please," you said to Ryan. You stood just inside the shop door. He went inside.

She was crying when she appeared with her case. You took it and went without saying anything out into the rain.

"Why are you crying, Joan?"

"They made me feel so awful going."

"Did they do anything to you?"

"No. They never spoke a word to me after you left. They made remarks among themselves. They didn't as much as shake hands there now."

"It doesn't matter. It's over. You're going home. People like that aren't worth cursing, never mind thinking about them. So just forget it. You'll never have to see them again."

Rain dripped from the lintel above the doorway you stood in, waiting for the bus to come.

Once you'd got the tickets in the bus she said, "What do you think he'll say?"

"He'll say nothing. I'll just tell him what happened. You couldn't stay on and that's all."

"What'll I do then? Where'll I go next?"

She might have asked the same question for yourself—for the first time you really looked in her face.

"I don't know. Stay at home for a while."

"But he'll make it awful."

"Go to England I suppose then."

"Will I have to go to England? It'll be horrid to face into all that strangeness." Her eyes were asking to relieve some of the oppression, the despair. She watched people leave and board the bus with the same impassiveness with which she watched the raindrops slip down the bleared windows.

"We may be all in England soon."

"You, too?"

"Me too," you smiled cruelly.

"But are you going to leave soon?"

"No. I don't think so but June isn't far away—and the exams."

"But you'll get a good job here?"

"There aren't many jobs."

"But you've a good chance?"

"Oh, Joan, it doesn't matter a curse. What the hell difference does it make? What the hell difference does anything make? We'll always be in some bus or something or room or road and air in our ears while we're in it no matter what happens."

Her questioning, her fear exasperated you to that. Now you saw how she drew away from your violence, that was not what she needed, and it was only with someone simple and weak you were able to be violent or in your own walled head but you weren't very violent with the priest two nights before.

"So we're going home, Joan." You placed your hand quickly on the back of her hand. "We'll have the great honour and joy of meeting our beloved father soon."

"Aye," she began to smile.

"So you're home, are you? Where's the food going to come outa to fill extra bellies. God, O God, O God, what did I do to deserve this cross? The poor-house, it's the poor-house ye'll all wind up in, and ye needn't say I didn't warn ye."

"O God, what did I do to deserve such a pack?" she took up shyly but laughing.

"Only for ye have your eejit of a father to come home to what would ye do? Then such thankless bastards the sun never saw."

"The poor-house, the poor-house, the poor-house," the girl was suddenly mimicking with real gaiety, taken out of herself, rocking with laughter when you took up where she stopped.

17

THERE WAS THAT MOMENTARY SILENCE OF SURPRISE WHEN they entered the kitchen by the back way and without knocking, opening slow the doors for warning. The evening meal was on the tables. They stood at the door, waiting for some reception, afraid.

"Joan, you're home," Mahoney was slow with surprise. He rose and took her hands and she kissed him, "You're welcome."

"Joan. Joan. Joan's home," the army of children showed a shouting of delight on their faces, but it was suppressed, because of their father's presence. They gathered shyly round her, she was the attraction. No one had ever been away for so long before. She'd a half-pound of cream caramels for them too.

"You're in the right time for the food," the father laughed

and soon they were at the tables, porridge of Indian meal, coarse and golden, dissolving in fine grains in the mouth, its delicate watery flavour drowned by the cream; and afterwards potatoes with buttered soda bread, and tea.

"It's a long time since you got the Indian meal," he joked, he seemed delighted. The scent of apples roasting in the baking-oven filled the kitchen, the hollow scooped in their centres full of melted sugar, and their green jackets turning to the yellow of butter. They were eaten as cards were played in the long evening afterwards, the father did not go out to the fields again though there was light, he took delight in the roasted apples and the playing.

"We'll have pains in our bellies tonight after these apples. Do you know, I'm like a perfessor now," he laughed, emphatically mispronouncing, as he rakishly dealt the cards, a pencil behind his ear, the sheet of foolscap on which he kept the scores by his elbow on the table.

"Sit on it. Wallop it," he shouted every time a trump made a tentative appearance. "Whatever else you do, keep the top man down."

"Ah, lucky card," he called out caressingly when the easy fall trick came his way.

The lamp was lit late. The night went unnoticed in this flash of happiness. The children, and Joan with them, went smiling to bed after he'd kissed them good night.

"This night you're home and safe at last," he kissed Joan.

Only when they'd all drifted to their rooms and Mahoney sat dealing out cards of patience did the night change to uneasiness and problems.

"Joan's home," he mused.

"She's home."

"You didn't stay long yourself with the Reverend Gerald?" he did not look up, crouched over the cards spread on the soft green surface of the table.

"No. There was no point."

"Things went badly so?"

"They didn't go very well."

"It's not on holidays Joan is home, is it?"

"No."

"Did anything happen?" his voice was low and probing, his hands moving the cards on the table, their corners flicking deliberately away. The silence and the tautness grew intense —white moths fluttered about the globe of the lamp.

"She was afraid. Ryan was interfering with her. She couldn't stay, it was I made her come home."

"How was he interfering with her?" the playing stopped for the first time, the eyes left the cards to search.

"As a girl. Sexually."

"Did he do her any harm?"

"No. I don't think so."

He felt what had happened as an accusation, the face darkened with hostility.

"What'll she do now?"

"I don't know."

"Stay here and wear the arse off herself sitting on chairs?"

"No."

"There's not enough of you as it is to feed, is there? How could anyone do anything with such a pack about him?"

"She can go to England."

It halted Mahoney. Slowly he gathered the cards into a solid pack.

"Go on the streets, is it?"

"She could train to be a nurse."

"But England's rotten, full of filth and dirt. No girl could be safe there."

"She wasn't very safe where she's after coming from and it's no England," it brought it to a sour enough end. Mahoney unlaced his boots, then quenched the lamp.

"It's time for bed," he said and as he turned away he asked tentatively, "What about yourself? How did things go between you and the priest?"

"I'm not going on to be a priest," it came to his own ears strangely as it sounded in the darkness that took on the quality of brooding night when Mahoney no longer moved. It was hard to believe the words he'd said were final yet.

The father began to say something but stopped. The cockroaches were boldly coming out of their holes, sense of them crawling from all walls in the darkness, the moving mass of legs carrying the shining shells of their backs, black and reddish brown. When Mahoney moved one of them cracked under his loose boots.

"May God direct you. Go to your bed now. There's no use hanging over the rakings in the dark.

18

ONE LONG GRIND OF STUDY FACED YOU THROUGH THAT WINTER
if you were to get anywhere in the exams and the kitchen was
no place for concentration. Preparing of meals or washing,
someone sweeping the floor, the squabbles and the games of
the children. Mahoney was hammering, the sharp crack of
sprigs driven in, and the grating of the rasp on leather, confused into the moral character of Henry of Navarre. The will
loosened. The page got blank, easier far to watch the shining
balls of metal run hissing from the iron when he soldered an
old saucepan. The guilt that you sat over books while he
slaved into the night was driven home to the quick.

"Get the sprigs. We want to be finished before morning.
We have to work. We can't be planked over a book. We have
to work."

The blow sank in and brought blood to the face but there

was too much control. The eyes slowly came up from the page and watched the large hands hammering. They bent down again with the half bitterness of a smile, they noted and kind of understood and they did not forgive, it was no house for reasonableness. You could only be silent and bow to it with as much detachment as you could get, and it might be right as anywhere else, it was simply the way the world was here, one day there might possibly be ferocity, but it was not to be this day.

When Mahoney was away they'd want to play: the rollicking blind-man's-buff, chairs going over, everything in danger, the wild rushes of the blind man and the escaping. No matter how you tried resentment rose, and you cried at them in rage.

"Can you not go easy? How can I get much work done in that racket?"

They'd stop, go to their places or schoolbags, sit in suppression. You were their tyrant in place of Mahoney now, and you'd be too disturbed after to be able to concentrate again.

"Go on. Play away," you'd get up in frustration and close the books, peace gone for that evening, and you'd watch them wary of you till they'd forget and grow intent as animals on their game, lost in the lamplight.

Impossible not to watch the slow hopscotch, whether the throw would find the chalked square, whether the piece of slate would remain steady on the head and hopping toe, fascination of eternal chance. Impossible too to refuse the invitation to join, see whether concentration and skill would defeat the limitations and traps, just for one game that so easily became several. The excitement of the danger of Mahoney coming never far, the slate picked up, the chalk marks obliterated by the wet brush kept handy, he'd have no chance to nag.

"Everything quiet of a sudden when I come, too quiet for

good," but there was nothing he could prove, they'd confront his suspicion with simple blankness.

No work much was got done. The weeks were going wasted.

"Can the man not keep quiet? Can he not sit? How can I go on? I must be going crazy," you cursed, a night in late October, the kitchen hot and crowded, Mahoney's hammer going ring-cling-cling on the rim of the bucket, the books useless on the table.

You might as well give up for good. It was useless trying. It was either give up, or go to one of the bedrooms upstairs where there was quiet. You'd freeze to death in those rooms without a fire, and to ask him for a fire was sure to rise trouble, but you were too driven desperate to care.

"I'm not able to study in this kitchen."

"Why? What's wrong with it?" he was immediately suspicious as always.

"There's too much noise. I just amn't able to concentrate."

"I thought that if you had your mind enough on what you're doing you'd be able to hear nothing else."

"No. I can't. The noise is driving me crazy."

"Well, we can't go round on tiptoe just for the one person. There's too much to do in this house, things to fix, too much work to do, and it can't be put on one side."

"There'd be no need. I could do the study in one of the rooms upstairs, there's an extra lamp."

"It's not the summer, you know."

"We could put a fire down."

"That'd be an extra fire in the house, wouldn't it?"

"It would but it'd be only for a few hours. We could put it in your room. It'd take the damp out of the walls. You're always saying it's the coldest room in the house," there was need for cunning once waste of money was in the air.

"So it is! It'd give you your death, that room would."

"We can put the fire there then, it'd be killing two birds that way."

"You might as well so if it's that important but I'm telling you it'll be all for nothing," he consented. "And remember we can't be going to Arigna for coal if the turf and sticks run out."

The fire was lit each evening in the room, the globe cleaned, the lamp lit. You'd sit at the table between the fire and the brass bells of the bed and read and write, the oil-lamp burning above the quiet books, the clock ticking, and the room warm with the fire. Downstairs the racket went on, but it was far away, remote as the wind in the winter outside. Each night you had a set amount of work to get through. You willed to do it perfectly, though the calm act of sitting down at the table never came easy. You'd find books to fiddle with or poke the fire into flame or wander away on any dream or distraction. It was a kind of tearing the sitting down. Once you were working you didn't mind, you didn't think of any outside world, the first breaking of the ice to be calm and sit was the worst.

You had to grind to do well in June. It could only be done a night at a time. You didn't know what you wanted to do with your life even if you did do well in June. June was as blank and distant as your death, with hot days perhaps. The only way to get release was to work. You'd not go down or stand aside, you'd ride on top of the others if you could, whatever security that'd give. It was too grisly to think, it was easier to work than to think. Death was all that mattered, it gave quickness, that was one accent you'd never lose. You didn't have to say it out loud. Life was the attraction, every instinct straining its way, and it was whether to be blind and follow, and work was a way out. Pass the exam. Learn the formula. Things would come out that way.

One-two-three-four the reasons Napoleon failed at Waterloo. Get by heart passages of prose to support an answer to Addison's style when you knew every characteristic of style except that it was simply the inexplicable way a man who usually donned britches in the mornings had of writing. Learn how to praise the sensuous mysticism, the haunting lyricism of *Ode to the Nightingale* if they asked for an appreciation: how Keats's imagination was befogged by too much heavy sensuousness if a criticism was the order of the day. On and on, further rubbish by the ton, cram it into the skull, get a high place in the Exam, play up and play the game well, ride down the slowcoaches.

You'd rise hot and tired from it all at ten, worn out. Pleasant to gather slowly then the books for the morning and quench the lamp, go down and look at the scrubbed raw boards of the table and linger over a cup of tea. The mind was drained, it wanted no more than to look at the solidity of things in tiredness and contentment. It had worked well. It could do no more. That was a kind of satisfaction that was hard to lose before sleep.

"Did you open the window before you came down? Not to have the room stinkin' with bad air."

"I did," the aggression couldn't even grate.

"How long were you up there tonight?"

"Four hours."

"It's alright till we'll have a doctor's bill on our hands, then we'll see. Then we'll see."

"That's the time the Superior says we should do."

"What does he care, what does he care? He'll not have to worry if you get sick."

What use was there answering, you were at peace. Let him continue, let him come to his own stop, let him rave till he choked.

"It's me has to do everything while you're at the school all day and up there with a fire at your arse all night. Will the

114

turf last out to the summer at that going? That's the question. Do you think we can afford to get coal from Arigna?"

"It doesn't burn that much. I can pay you back," the resolution to stay clear of conflict didn't last long.

"You'll pay me back. I'd like to see that. Where's the money coming outa? Nineteen damned near and not a round copper earned yet."

"I'll be finished in a few months."

"We'll be all finished in a few months be the look of things or in the poor-house or somewhere. What'll you do when you're finished—walk round with your hands in your pockets like the other gents about that went to college."

"I can get a job."

"Ye'll not all get jobs, that's certain shooting. Only the ones with the pull will get the jobs."

"If you're good enough you'll get a job."

"There seems an awful lot about not good enough then. You'll be the outstanding one, of course."

"I can go to England and pay you back from there."

"Anyone can go to England. You don't have to waste years at school to go to England. If you've a fiver in your pocket and the boat fare you can go to England, that's all that's wanting. And I don't want any dirty money from England. What do I want your money for? I got on before I ever saw sight or light of you, and I'll get on after. Who wants your cursed money?"

Violence had grown, steady eye on his throat and talking face, urge to smash him. Hate gave such strength that you felt you could break him, you didn't care about anything any more, there was only this doghouse of the teeth at the throat.

"Can you not shut up? Can you not even leave me alone for these few months?" you cried violently into his face and Mahoney was taken back, he could not meet it with his own old violence.

"Look. Look at you now, the eyes gone mad. In the lunatic asylum you'll wind up, that's what your study will do," he mocked when he recovered. "No one's doing anything to you. Of course as usual make a mountain out of a molehill. You can have as much peace as'll burst you in this house."

"Alright, will you just, just leave me alone?" you shouted and went hurrying outside before he had time to answer. You heard him turn in sudden fury on some of the others as you closed the door.

You were crying. No one else in the class had to put up with such as this. They'd be helped and encouraged to study, not this mess, with that bastard of a madman shouting and hammering and abusing away, and why had you to be given such a dog's chance.

Your feet were on the mould of the rhubarb bed going for the lavatory with its Jeyes Fluid and solitary airhole when you stopped. You couldn't do it, go in and smother yourself with sympathy and cursing.

What happened didn't matter, you had to go on, that was all. You had to look it in the face. That was the way your life was happening, that was the way you were. There was no time for sadness or self-pity. The show of your life would be always moving on to the next moment. The best was to dress up and bow to it and smile or just look on but it was easier to say than do.

The night was cold. Away towards Oakport, above the Limekiln Wood, you began to watch the clouds cross the face of the three-quarter moon.

19

The next night you didn't give up, you'd go through in the face of set teeth before you'd give up now or be crushed by some other force outside your own will. You forced yourself down to Stamp's account of the Black Earth belt of Russia, underlining as you went, pausing to go back over. When it was finished you shut the book and with savage gloating whispered the account point by point into the night of the bedroom. A grim smile over Virgil. This was the slow night of struggle, night after night till June, and the strain couldn't be much worse in life afterwards. You'd the satisfaction of staggering away from it downstairs at ten, completely worn, the swaying contentment after the football pitch or alley, only more so, diabolical pride of drawing the mind to the boundaries of what it could take, the shiver of the nerves as it trembled back from the edges.

Violence often came: frustrated abuse of the books on the table till your hand hurt or you got afraid the noise might carry downstairs; or desire to smash the lamp would end with you going to the bed, loosening your clothes. A newspaper down on the floor, pull up the draped eiderdown, press your flesh on the bed's edge. Black hair and lips on the yellow coverlet; soft white of the breast, pink nipple, lower. Pump your nakedness into the bed's belly, hot flush rushing to the face as it goes down to the lips opening and closing on the yellow coverlet, the raw tongue seeking past the teeth, fit of trembling before the seed pumps rustling down on the already positioned newspaper. Heavy breathing and sweat hampers the dressing again. Crumple the newspaper and put it to burn, the wet centre hissing. You are quiet and moping, the body dead as ashes: as you go back to the table and books a vicious musing about how many conceptions the rationed distribution of all that seed hissing in the centre of the newspaper, how many could it cause, the passing eggs touched to life.

The house exam was held at Christmas, trial run before the summer. It'd decide who'd continue in the honours course, who'd leave off to concentrate on passing, and passing was no good to you. You had to get high in the honours to stand a chance in the cut-throat competition for the Scholarships or E.S.B. or Training College or anything. Passing was only good if you had your own money to go to the University and few at the school had that. Most came from small farms in the country on their bicycles, stacked downstairs where they ate their lunches out of paper bags and horseplayed on wet days. They knew too it was get high honours or go to England. The air was tense with this fear through the exam, the folding doors that separated the classrooms drawn back to make an examination hall.

This was the first time you'd ever thoroughly prepared for

118

an exam, and it was strange excitement to be familiar with every question, able to answer it more completely than the time allowed—all the evenings with the tin oil-lamp and the fire fusing here in mastery, feeling of absolute surefootedness, and then you were simply writing, watching the electric clock close to the crucifix on the wall, the three hours gone in a flash. Down in the bicycle room you went over the questions with the others—did you get this for that, what did you put down for No. 5—elation and disappointment but your answering was as irrevocably fixed as a life that has run its course. Better far to forget it, take off the coats and make for the handball alley. Arrange an even doubles, you and O'Reilly against Moran and Monaghan. Excitement and striving reduced the world to the concrete walls and the netting wire behind, the white lines on the concrete floor, the rubber with its Elephant brand that was driven and driven again against the wall as the aces fell away towards defeat or victory at twenty-one.

Holly with red berries was got from Oakport; ivy nearer home, for the bare walls. Fruit and some Santa Claus presents for the younger children came from town. Joan made a plum pudding with the help of the yellowed cookery-book. Though Mahoney took little part in these preparations he did not complain when they asked him for the extra the few luxuries cost, and on Christmas Eve he made his own strange gesture to the festival.

"Do you know what I think? I think we should give the Brothers something for Christmas."

"But you never gave anything before."

"No, but it's your last Christmas at school. They've done a lot for you. It's only right to show some appreciation."

"What are you going to give?"

"I was thinking we could do worse than give them two good bags of spuds—two bags of the Golden Wonders."

"It's cigarettes or whiskey that's usually given," you tried to tell but he'd made up his mind. There was no use arguing. The potatoes were worth a bottle of whiskey but he could make a present of the potatoes without feeling the pain of parting with actual money.

"Well what do you think?" he was demanding.

"I suppose you better give the Golden Wonders so," there was nothing else to say.

He found two new meal-bags and you helped him fill the bags out of the short Golden Wonder pit, the clay on its sides frozen hard as concrete, having to be broken with the spade. Afterwards dressed up and on his way to town Mahoney was very happy, not aware much of the freezing blue Christmas Eve, shouting at everyone that passed, and humming over and over "Christmas is coming the geese are getting fat", while you sat ashamed, hot at how the potatoes and Mahoney would seem to the cool Benedict, in the stupidity of youth.

The embarrassment had grown almost to sickness by the time you'd to walk with Mahoney down the concrete path between the white lawn blocks and knock on the monastery door.

"We wondered if we could see Brother Benedict," Mahoney asked the maid, a young girl with a pale nervous face.

"The Brothers are on retreat, but you go to the school, don't you?" she said.

"Yes. That's right," Mahoney answered, and she put you in the parlour, and struck the brass gong once in the hallway to call Benedict, the single stroke because he was the Superior. Soon the sound of his *crêpe* shoes and soutane were on the stairs from the oratory.

"We're sorry. We didn't know about the retreat," Mahoney apologized as they shook hands.

"It's annual, it ends this evening, and it's alright. Even retreats have to allow for human troubles or business," Benedict smiled his cool ironic smile, with the eyes.

120

"No, there's no trouble," Mahoney was very uncertain. "We brought some potatoes for Christmas. We wondered where you'd like us to put them."

"That's very kind of you. Thank you. We can bring them round to the potato-shed at the back," and the only change was that the smile seemed for a moment to take on more energy as he spoke. He got the bunch of keys and showed the way to the sheds at the back, where the cabbage garden and orchard and alley was. You emptied them on the floor with Mahoney, who took both the empty bags away.

"Our friend here has shown remarkable improvement. He carries our chief hopes this year in the examination," Benedict referred to you as the bags were emptied.

"Well he works enough anyhow," Mahoney was as uncertain, as embarrassed as you, it was strange.

"It was most generous of you to bring us the potatoes," Benedict said at the gate, after five minutes of crucifying attempts at conversation around the sheds, no one at ease or knowing what to say.

"We wanted to show our appreciation," Mahoney said and then tried to escape this unaccustomed burden of politeness by joking, "The old potato helps to keep the wind out of all our stomachs, doesn't it?"

"It does indeed," it seemed from Benedict's smile and ironic agreement that he was dangling Mahoney's words before his face in the cold, was sniffing them with the most exquisite nostrils, as he would a dead field-mouse. "It fills many a vacuum. I often think anybody writing a work on our character as a nation would have to closely investigate the influence of the same potato," there was the cut of amusement in his voice.

"There was the famine the once it failed," Mahoney was easier, and proud. He did not notice.

"Well we're well provisioned against it this year," Benedict smiled, and it was cold at the gate. "You were very kind. A happy Christmas to you both," he put out his hand.

"A happy Christmas, Brother," it was over, and you went with the two meal-bags between the shops, holly and fairy lights in the windows, a huge Christmas-tree at the Clock. People were hailing each other and going together for drinks, the pubs noisy and bright with coal fires, Murray's and the Railway Bar.

"Nothing lacking except the snow," Mahoney said as you left. "Those Brothers earn their salvation, up there praying with all this going on, and that Benedict is very clever. You can tell."

You made some formal noise of agreement and wondered if Benedict would keep the potatoes or flog them for whiskey but you said nothing. And you had to think as you went with Mahoney home that if you passed the exams, and married, the fate it would be to have to walk with a son as taciturn and withdrawn as you now. It'd be real nightmare. You listened to Mahoney talk and talk. No matter what else, he had at least the beauty of energy.

He was in the front field when the postman brought the exam result after Christmas, it was addressed to him as parent, but neither would it have made difference if it hadn't, he still opened every letter that came to the house no matter who it was addressed to. When he took it inside he tried to adopt a mannered casualness.

"Congratulations. You walked away with first place. All I hope is that it doesn't give you a swelled head."

"He's gone completely ahead of the class and at this rate of progress there's nothing he may not attain to," he read.

Your hands trembled as they accepted the report sheet, tears of gratitude and resultant generosity that you couldn't hold back. You'd been praised and you wished to return it, praise the whole world, but once you looked deeper there was the discomfort of an accusation, what right had you to take praise, you had none, what right had Benedict to praise you, but joy trampled it down, it was good to take it no matter what it was.

"If you do as well in the summer we'll have cause for real celebration," Mahoney said.

"Thanks," what more was there to say.

"Me and Pat Flynn were always neck-and-neck for top place in the National School. The last year, seventh class, I got the first," he was moved enough to speak out of his own life.

"Where is Pat Flynn now?" you had to ask, to pretend an interest.

"He's dead. He went on to Moyne and to be a priest for the Missions. In Africa he died. He was home once but I missed him. A great man to kick a point from the wing too. He died shortly after going out the second time, the White Man's Grave it's called," he said and wandered a second in reflection.

"And, do you know, I'm here, if anyone's interested," he resumed with strange humour.

"Who'd ever believe except myself that I'm here," he chuckled harshly as he went out again towards the front field.

The small smell of success made a change in Mahoney to the study alone in the room. It was no longer an unhealthy and suspicious activity, wasting light and fuel but possibility of the world now, attractive labels of esteem and money close. His curiosity was as much roused by it now as the enigma of the hopeless struggle in loneliness had roused his mistrust before. He would share it this way.

"What'll happen if you do walk away with the exams?"

"I could get a Scholarship."

"How many are there?"

"Two for the County."

"But there'll be a lot in for them?"

"Some hundreds."

"That's a lot to have to trounce. But say, say if you got it, what could you do?"

"You could go to the University, study for whatever you'd want."

"What do you think you'd go for?"

You didn't know. The University was a dream: not this slavish push in and out through wind and rain on a bicycle, this dry constant cramming to pass the exam, no time to pause to know and enjoy anything, just this horrid cram into the brain to be forgotten the minute the exam was over. Though there were mornings, the hawthorns becoming green and no one on the early road and you could shout *The Ode to Virgil* for joy as you pedalled: evenings after football, the delicious weariness and warmth, but nothing seemed to have anything much got to do with school.

The University would be different, you'd seen pictures, all stone with turrets surrounded by trees, walks between the lawns and trees, long golden evenings in the boats on the Corrib. You'd be initiated into mystery. If you went for medicine, the parts of the body you'd know, the functions, the structure of the mystery. All day you could pore over the marvel and delight of the books of the world if you chose the arts. You could walk under trees and talk with men and women who were initiates with you too, men your own age, and walk with a girl of your own who was studying the same as you.

"I don't know. There are too many things."

"You might even do medicine?"

"I might," it was growing disturbing, too real in the other mind, and it was so far away and unlikely.

"If you kept passing the exams you'd get more scholarships. You could be a specialist or surgeon then. You could wind up in Harley Street. That's what'd be a big shake-up for some around here—if you wound up in Harley Street!"

"I got no Scholarship yet. It's a chance just."

"A chance, hundreds in for it," he repeated glumly, the castles fallen. "You've no pull."

"It's not the pull, it's the marks, if I get high enough of marks I'll get it."

"Are you soft enough to think the marks can't be fiddled if you've got the pull. You're very young in the world, you'll learn a sore thing or two yet. I could tell you a thing or two for the amount of schooling I got and that's one of them," it had to come to some end.

Trouble about the fire and light was gone, Mahoney's interference changed to concern over the relentless studying.

"You're burning the midnight oil too low, I'm telling you. Enough is as good as a feast. You'll do harm to yourself."

"It's only for another few months."

The bones stood out clear in the face in the mirror, a sunken glow in the eyes.

"They broke stronger men than you, the same books," atavistic fear was in the eyes that looked on the quiet books on the table in the lamplight. "Far stronger men than you the books broke. And if you haven't your health what good will it all do you?"

"I feel alright."

"You'll feel alright when you're in a brown box too, not a care in the world on you, let others do the worrying and the burying."

The best was to stand there and say nothing, the less his idea was opposed the more quickly it'd wear itself out.

"You'll probably wind up with nothing in the heel of the hunt anyhow. You'll look a right eejit then, won't you? And don't say I didn't warn you. But I suppose there's people dying that never died before," and he went muttering out of the house.

20

School went in grinding concentration on June, what questions were most likely to be asked and how to answer, practice at the papers of previous years, ideal answers from Caffrey's Correspondence College in Dublin.

The only interruptions were the priests from the various orders in search of vocations. Once or twice in these appeals they phrased your own torment too close for comfort.

"My dear boys, you are on the threshold of life, a life that'll end in death. Then the Judgment. All the joys and pleasures of life you yearn for now will have been just a passing bauble then. If you clutch at these now will they avail you anything in the only important moment in life, moment of death? On the other hand, if you give your life to God, and surely the priesthood is the gift outright, you can say you kept nothing back. As your whole life was in God, so will your life be in death, and in the hereafter."

That was it simply, and you had set your face the other way from it, towards the bauble. You were heading out into an uncertain life, sacrificing the certainty of a life based on death; for what you didn't know, windblown excitements and imaginings that in the humdrum of their actuality might soon get stripped of their sensual marvel.

How easy it would be to go downstairs to the community room where the priest interviewed anyone interested afterwards and say: "I want to become a priest, father." Everything would be taken care of. You'd go on to the Seminary at the end of the year. You'd be cut loose from your father. You'd not have to worry about a job or what people thought. In your death you'd be a priest, a priest of God, the death already accepted in life, the life already given into His keeping before it was required, years before, in your youth.

You'd be almost afraid to look at the leaflet handouts the priest took from the black leather case afterwards, photos of the Seminary life, on the football pitch and in the oratory, happily eating in the refectory, bent in the peace of books at study, walking with companions through grounds filled with evergreens.

There was a fierce drag to go down to the community room and give your life into that death, but no, you'd set your face another direction, and you knew if you did go down that the drag would be back to where you were now. No way was easy.

The other appeals—comradeship, the sharing of mysterious power, working in exotic countries where oranges and lemons grew along the roadside, walking with the great of the land—never moved you much. In the reality your life moved in the shade of a woman or death. Only the lifeless or blind fell for the lesser than these. This was just the destruction of

127

entering the dream around delight of the woman or the disciplined waiting in the priesthood of Christ.

Mahoney's violence was turning more on himself. He came reeking with Guinness from the April market. When they'd given him his meal, answered his inquiries about the pigs and milking, and he could find nothing to fault, he let himself slump before the heat of the fire. It seemed he'd doze quietly there. Then suddenly he jumped up, the face red and bloated, dramatic arm outstretched, to do a half-circle swing on the floor and shout, "I went to school too."

"This is my life, and this kitchen in the townland of Cloone is my stage, and I am playing my life out here on," and he stood, the eyes wild, as if grappling for his lines.

"And nobody sees me except a crowd of childer," the voice trailed bitterly, and then burst out again.

"But it's important, it's important to me, it's the only life I've got, it's more important than anything else in the world to me. I went to school too," and he started to sob drunkenly till he grew aware of the still eyes of the children watching him, when he began to shout again.

"What are ye gaping at? Have you nothing to do but stand with your mouths open? Such a useless pack," and they instinctively scattered, years of habit, before he could single any one of them out.

As June drew closer the school prayers, morning and evening, were offered for the exams—that the school might do well. The class was exhorted to offer their private prayers for the same intention.

Please God may I not fail.

Please God may I get over sixty per cent.

Please God may I get a high place.

Please God may all those likely to beat me get killed in road accidents, and may they die roaring.

It made no sense, even if you did say your prayers any

more. If God was there nothing mattered but the Presence.

The poor, the tramps of the road, were supposed to have better chance in the final round-up than the secure. What was you alone went to Him, not roses and vegetable garden and semi-detached house and young wife and children and the Ford or Volkswagen for Sunday outings from the Dublin suburbs you took to him if you got the Junior Executive Exam for the Civil Service, but whatever was you alone.

What was there to do but keep silent, but when Mahoney offered the hurried rosary they said each night for your success you couldn't stand it, at least Mahoney should be above that slobber, you thought.

"What did you say that for?" you almost shouted the moment they'd finished, unable to choke back the anger.

"What?"

"Praying for my success."

"Don't you want the Grace of God or are you a pagan or something?"

"No. It's not that. What does it matter to God whether I get the exam or not, or to my life under him? If it's his Will, and I'm lucky enough and good enough, I'll get the exam. And if I don't it doesn't matter. It'll not matter the day I'm dying."

"What sort of rubbish and blasphemy am I listening to?"

"None. You want to use prayer like money, wheedle the exam out of God. Can't you leave it alone. God is more important than a getter of exams for people. What does it matter whether I get the exam or not?"

"There was enough fire and light used on it then, if it wasn't important. You should take your scarecrow face and bag of bones before a mirror if you want to get a fright sometime, apparently it matters that much. And now you're gone too crazy madhouse to ask God. Is it out of your mind you're gone?"

"No. I'm sane as you are, or more. Ask for Grace if you want, but don't ask him to pass the exam——"

"Heathen rubbish!"

"No. No exam deserves the Grace of God, nobody does. Let them ask Grace, a bolloksed poor devil, but no, no, no."

Mahoney waited till the rush of passion subsided, and then addressed more the general house than made direct answer.

"Do you hear what I had to wait till near the end of my days to hear in my own house? Heathen rubbish. And in future keep your dirty language for your street-corner friends in town, do you hear me?"

"I do, but I don't want any praying for exams."

"We wouldn't as much as dirty prayers with your name again but such filth and rubbish. Hell is where you're heading for and fast. I never knew too much books to do good yet. Puffed pride. You think you can do or say anything you've a mind for. I've seen a few examples of it in me time, but never such prize heretic baloney as this night. I'll hear no more in this house. Do you hear me now?"

"Alright. You'll hear no more."

"Such rubbish," he went on complaining. "And in front of the children too. Puffed up and crazy, it'd choke you to live the same as other people, wouldn't it? You don't even need God now? You wouldn't ever have to do such a mean thing as clean your arse, would you, these days? Maybe it's up in the sky you spend your time these days, having conversations with God, and not down here with the likes of us. And I reared you and let you to school for that. As if there could be luck in a house with the likes of you in it."

He went muttering and complaining that way to bed. And then, when he was gone, the wave of remorse that came. You'd troubled him, and for what? Did it matter what was prayed for? If it gave him satisfaction to pray for success why not let him, it would make no difference except he'd not be upset as now. Stupid vanity had caused it all. The house had gone to bed. You were alone in the kitchen. You wanted to say to him you were sorry but you weren't able.

His boots, wet from the grass, stood drying by the raked fire. They started to take on horrible fascination.

They were your father's boots, close to the raked fire. They'd been put there to dry for morning. Their toes touched where the ashes spilled out from the fire on the concrete, boots wet from the grass. Your father's feet had been laced in their black leather, leather over walking flesh. They'd walk in his hopes, be carried over the ground, till they grew worn, past mending, and were discarded for the new pair from Curley's, on and on, over the habitual fields, lightly to the football matches in Reegan's field on Sundays, till the feet themselves wore, boots taken off his dying feet. Corns of the flesh against the leather. All the absurd anxiety and delight and heedlessness the boots carried. They stood so utterly quiet by the fire, the feet that they'd cover resting between sheets to wear them through another day. The boots were so calm there. They would not move. You touched them in fascination, they did not stir, only the rough touch of wet boot leather against the finger-tips. One lace was broken, replaced by white twine.

How could you possibly hurt or disturb anyone? Hadn't the feet that wore the boots, all that life moving in boot leather, enough to contend with, from morning to night to death, without you heaping on more burden, from sheer egotism. Did it matter to the boots, moving or still, whether your success was prayed for or not? Why couldn't you allow people to do the small things that pleased them? In this same mood you did what you had never done and went and knocked on his door.

"Who's that? What do you want?"

"I'm sorry over the prayers."

131

"It's a bit late in the day to be sorry now, easy to be sorry when the harm's done, such heathen rubbish, easy to know why you're sorry. It's more than sorry you ought to be——"

Anger rose as the voice continued to complain out of the darkness of the bedroom. The same boots could kick and trample. You couldn't stand it, you'd only meant well, that was all.

"Forget it for God's sake. I just said I was sorry," you said and closed the door sharply to go troubled and angry through the kitchen to your own bedroom.

21

CLOSER AND CLOSER THE EXAM CAME ON A COUNT OF DAYS, early June days of pure summer that year, memory of boats on the river down the town at the bridge and girls in white at tennis over by the Courthouse on Wednesday half-days through dead evenings. All but the exam classes had been let away on summer holidays. The pressure of the ordinary schooldays was completely relaxed, effort to ease the strain of waiting for the exam. Timetable and rule went overboard, chairs were brought out on the lawn. In the shade of the huge cypress tree a half-circle was made about Benedict, the lawn bright outside the shade, white flags of the clock golf, white lawn blocks like toy dogs on either side of the concrete path that cut the lawn in two, the pink snow of petals on the grass under the one lilac tree.

"There's no need to sweat any more. The work is over. More harm than good is always done this time of year by work. Just relax. An exam is the same as a football match. You never train heavily on its eve. What we'll do now is go over any points that still puzzle you. Well, I'm waiting for questions," Benedict smiled, the jet-black hair sleeked, he'd to shave twice a day because of the darkness of his beard. The wide leather belt was buckled tight about the narrow waist, part of the cape drawn across his throat and thrown over his shoulder. It was said that he could read in six languages and that he had foreign blood because of his blackness.

Questions moved about the Council of Trent, a point of grammar in one of the Horace Odes, Plantation of Ulster, degenerating into sheer time-wasting and ease in the end.

"Do you think if Horace came he'd understand the Latin the way we read it?"

"No. He'd probably be horrified. But you needn't fear, McDermott, the only ghosts you should have back these days are the nights you spent in the Gaiety all winter."

"Why is the dead language of Latin used in the Mass?"

"Because it's the official language of the Church, binding together the differences of so many languages, the universal unchanging language."

It was a game, not touching the exam.

A drill battered at concrete the other end of the town. Cars passed the gate on the Dublin Road, the stone Celtic cross above it, AD MAIOREM DEI GLORIAM. The shadow of the great cypress, stretching farther than the hedge of flowering currant and the high wall, stayed still on the lawn. The questions lazed on.

"Were the Romans much like us?"

"Why were so many of the poets heretics and mad?"

"How many classes have you prepared for the Leaving since you became a Brother?"

"Do you think has Roscommon much of a chance in the All Ireland this year?"

"Do you think our class is among the better or worse?"

You sat on that lawn through those questions, part of your life passed that way, in the ease of the day and this shuttlecock of undemanding question and answer. Though the ease was broken by constant flashes: the exam was near, the day of reckoning. A horrible tightening of fear gathered in the guts. Benedict said you'd walk away with the Scholarship, but there was always luck he said too.

Would you fail? Fail Benedict's opinion, not have any luck, get the wrong questions, not having what it took in the last round-up. You could hear your father's voice when that result came.

"See where the study got you after it all, the amount of fire and light down the drain, and for nothing. Yourself and the rest of the house damned near driven cracked. Didn't I tell you? I told you only those with the pull would get anything, didn't I tell you that?"

You tried to shut your eyes. Your eyes strayed about. Grass, concrete, shade, strands of wire running between concrete posts and beyond the sanded yard you used cross with the bicycle, all the times rough-and-tumble soccer was kicked there with a sponge ball. Fallen lilacs were on the lawn. A hit tune started to beat through the sickness: "We'll gather lilacs in the springtime."

They'd all gather lilacs in a horrible summertime, parched into dust. Dry lilac petals choking your father's mouth, your own mouth, rotting life of the lawn about the lilac tree, under the bridges of Paris with me, darling you'll hold me tight.

The sun, the heat was the worst. The futility of the chairs on the lawn. Your father might be right enough yet, you were half crazy. If you'd kept on to be a priest you'd be calm as the others; just an easy progression into a seminary of continuing days is all you'd have to fear.

"Security. Security. Security. Everyone's looking for security," the Reverend Bull Reegan shouted annually from the pulpit at every annual retreat.

Lives were lived through in this rathole of security, warding off blows, dealing blows, one desperate cling to stay alive in the rat hole; terror of change; neither much risk or generosity or praise, even madness as banal and harmless as anything else there. You must get the same bus at the same time on the same road each morning, hang your hat on the same hook, have three pennies for the same newspaper which the news-boy would hand you without you asking. That was the height of the exam. That of the recognition in the city when you'd walk out of the office with the umbrella.

Dream of a girl's mouth on the lawn in the cypress shade and Benedict's dry ironic voice yards away with the drill digging the concrete, no taking to the air a quiet breath without moan, but the last shiver of the nerves in soft threshing thighs and lips on a dancing floor.

No. Some ordinary futility instead, fail the exam, a second-class ticket on the nightboat for Holyhead, and did it matter, but it was too close to the exam to turn back, just go blindly into it for the next fortnight for God's sake.

"Pray for success. Ask God's blessing. Have the peace of the state of Grace in your soul. Put yourself as an instrument in God's hand. You'll not fare any worse by it," Benedict was saying, obviously ready to end the class, and it was no use to you.

"I have studied the course, worked as hard as I could drive myself. After that it's a game with luck. I'll just go in and do it as best I can. If anyone's better it has nothing to do with me. There's not places for everyone, only two, no matter how good the rest are. It's only a shocking game. And who are the judges and what are their standards anyhow?" you tried to phrase as you left the lawn with your books and chair.

"You can go to England if all fails. You'll work in Dagenham and they'll call you Pat."

"Will you make up a game for the alley," O'Reilly called, it was the best. A doubles, energy let loose in this striving, the concrete wall before you, imprisoned by the high netting wire. The small elephant was a brown blur of spin and speed. There was the joy of skill and pure movement, the flash of instinctive thinking, and it was of no consequence much who won or lost. Outside the netting wire was the mould of the monastery garden, full of cabbages and young potato stalks.

22

THE DAYS IMMEDIATELY BEFORE THE EXAM TOOK ON THE quality of a dream: time passing, the will paralysed, watching the certain flow towards the brink in helpless fear and fascination, it could not be true and yet it was drawing relentlessly close. Possibility of working was gone, the listless turning of pages I knew already by heart alone in the room. Evenings across Oakport towards the river with books; but, instead of studying, all it was possible to do was gaze at the great rusting gates of Oakport that used open to coaches once, the weathered white of the rotting wood of Nutley's boathouse, the reeds along the shore trembling with fish and the endless water. On the way home through the wood my feet tramping on the bluebells. The exam was only days away, but it was as unreal as my own death; was all life like this; and it was impossible to be easy. Crossing the stone walls of the Plains with the sheepdog in the hope of the distraction of a grazing rabbit was one escape.

The day before the exam was an intensification of the same, a Sunday, hot and without a breeze. With Joan I went on the river, in the old tarred boat, the tar melting and smelling in the heat, and I'd to pour water over the squealing rowing-pins. She let out the spoons and I rowed at slow trawling speed, but there was too much brightness, the light glaring off the water, not even in the shade of Oakport Wood along the edges of the drowning leaves did a single fish strike. Joan sat with the lines in her hands at the end of the boat. I rowed with the same mechanical slowness, lifting the oars high now and then to listen to the ripple of the boat through the glass-calm water.

"Are you worried about tomorrow?" she asked.

"I don't know. The whole business seems cuckoo or something. It's not real. Why did you ask?"

"No why. You didn't speak a word since we left. I was just wondering."

"I suppose I must be worried."

In a dream the boat went by the known landmarks. The Gut at the mouth between a red navigation pan and a black, the Golden Bush good for perch, Toughran's Island, Knock-vicar Island and the creamery through the trees, the three arches of Knockvicar Bridge with the scum from the creamery sewer along the sally bushes, names bedded for ever in my life, as eternal.

Knockvicar Locks was as far as the boat could get up the river, because of the great wooden gates. To an ash sapling rooted in the stones we tied the boat and started to worm fish for perch, an even mane of water falling across the wall and churning white out on the stones from the sluice, the smell of rotting river-weed thick in the air.

The place was almost crowded: a few boats, people sitting

on the lock gates or out on the wall fishing with their trousers rolled to their knees, the mane of water dragging at their ankles before it poured down the green wall; girls on the grass along the bank. There was sense of laziness and ease and Sunday over it all, but the fishing was without pleasure, listlessly pulling in the small perch, their bright red fins and the gills working on the floor of the boat till they died in the heat, baiting the hook again, and sitting to watch the cork. The exam was tomorrow, the first day would be finishing this time tomorrow, it wasn't possible to believe, and there was only a dull ache. This whole corner of river was a painting of a Sunday, even children. These hadn't to wrestle with any exams. They were as fixed here on hot Sundays as the river. There was no darkness or fear or struggle. Their cigarette-packets drifted past. Only a fool wanted to be different.

"I'm sorry, Joan. I can't stand it. We'll go home."

Rowing home was distraction, the sense of movement. I had at least the notion of going some place. Though before the boat was half-way I was worrying if the oars would blister my hands for the morning, it'd be almost safer to ask Joan to row.

"Tomorrow the exam starts," Mahoney echoed it at tea.

"Yes, tomorrow," I nodded. "Tomorrow and tomorrow and tomorrow," started to beat to the mind out of *Macbeth*.

"What subject is on?"

"It's Irish first."

"Don't worry, not to worry is the important thing. It's not an execution you're going for, remember. Cool, calm and collected, the three seas of wisdom and success."

The house grew impossible to endure, outside the glare was gone, a liquid yellow from the west pouring on the gates under the yew. I went by the orchard, the apples green and hard, the big rhubarb leaves crowding out of the wooden frame, the red stalk streaked with green when I lifted the

140

leaves. The fierce urge to touch grew, the pale moss on the apple branches with my finger-tips, brittle and hard; the cool of a rhubarb leaf against my face. The wooden stile at the bottom was white with weather, the bucket handle nailed into the yew to steady you over was cold. Nettles and huge dock grew choking against the thorn hedge except where the fowl scraped.

This place was at least green and real, I tried to say; but it wasn't possible for long. The exam was tomorrow. I couldn't face the exam. I'd have to go sick. I'd steal away to England. No, simply endure, it's enough, was argued back. I'm afraid in case I'll fail, and wreck my pride, and what does that matter. It's useless to run. It's the same stake as Macbeth's except for the banality of the whole situation. And it's fight a way out or go down. Everyone can't be king but it's the same. They have to fight their way out or go down. My hands clenched as they touched the bucket handle to cross the stile. I kicked at the harmless grasses.

It was impossible not to laugh too, it was too comic, the whole affair exaggerated, I was going to no crucifixion on a mountain between thieves but to a desk in a public building to engage in a writing competition. The whole business had grown out of proportion, though in a way why shouldn't it, I was at the heart of the absurdity and what proportion was there to my life, what did I know about it. I knew nothing.

It was as good to climb to the hay-shed across the meadow in the shelter and lie on the old hay. No one would come there. Lying on the bank of hay you could look over the miles of stone walls across the Plains towards Elphin. The smoke of Carrick clouded the sky far off on the left, changed in the light, and soft yellow.

The hay could stir promptings, the wenches that beat it out on their backs in hay-sheds under the waggoners of Jeffrey Farnol. The sharp ends pricked through clothes. I might as well, might as well finish the way I'd begun, what did it matter, why not, no one would come here. A girl in the hay, breasts and lips and thighs, a heart-shaped locket swinging in the valley of her breasts, I'd catch it with the teeth, the gold hard but warm from her flesh. The hay comes sharp against my skin once I get my trousers free. The miraged girl is in the hay, shaking hay in my eyes and hair, and she struggles and laughs as I catch her, and she yields, "My love," and folds my lips in a kiss. I lay her bare under my hands, I slide into her, the pain of the pricking hay delicious pleasure.

"My love. My love. My love," I mutter, the lips roving on the hay, the seed pumping free, and it was over. The blue sky over the Plains came to my raised eyes, the stone walls, the grazing sheep, small white birds in the distance between stones, the trunks of three green oaks at the top of the meadow, and the light between. Nothing was changed. Half stripped I lay on the hay, a dry depression settling, and I had to get up, the fixing of shirt and trousers on the height of hay absurd embarrassment. The seed was lost in the hay. It'd dry. A grim smile as I wondered a minute what it'd taste like to the cattle. Strange how human seed would only grow in humans, no good pumping it into either a mare or a mouse, they had their own seed.

I'd to hang round till I was calmer, brush my clothes clean. The exam was tomorrow. It was far away as tomorrow now, I didn't care. It was strange how there never was any urge towards abuse when I was at peace.

23

THE CLASS MET AT THE MONASTERY GATE, THOSE WHO HAD
bicycles parked them in the big room inside. Benedict came
with us up Gallows Hill to the Convent. No one spoke much.

"Remember to read down through the paper. Don't plunge
at the first question you know. Pick out the questions you
intend to answer. Allot a time to each. Spend ten minutes
picking the questions, it'll be well spent. And don't spend too
much time at any one question," Benedict gave last advice
outside the Convent, white railings round the lawns and
flowerbeds by the wall, and we were checking for the tenth
time if we had pen and ink and ruler, the card with the
number. If we could get a glance at what was on the paper
we'd give money or if there was any chance of escape.

The desks were arranged inside in the assembly hall, under
the stage the Superintendent stood, a green curtain with two
gold bands across. I found the desk with my number and sat.

The official black box was unlocked. The rules were read. Someone in the front desks witnessed the breaking of the seal on the envelope that held the papers. The papers were given out face downwards, red for honours, a blue paper for pass. I watched the clock. At ten I'd lift the red paper and read.

The hands that took it at ten were clumsy. The eyes read down the page, only half taking in what was there, but enough to tell that all the nights and concentration hadn't been for nothing. The desire to rush at the questions had to be beaten back. I picked the questions, marked what I'd picked, a quick glance at the other faces, and I became a writing machine, putting down what I'd learned the way they told me to, glancing up at the clock, once asking for more foolscap.

Unbelievably quick the three hours were at an end. I handed up the envelope and left. Benedict was outside on the gravel, a huddle about him going feverishly over the paper, the mistakes and the triumphs, how much better every one would do if it was possible to have one more go at it, what they'd avoid.

We went back to the monastery during the lunch hour, the interest changing to the next paper at two, what'd be on, and it was over at five. I was cycling home same as usual except more spent after the excitement. It hadn't been very terrible. Tomorrow would be another day, History, some things I wanted to go over to make fresh. That night was less restless, before the end of the fortnight it had grown much the same as ordinary schooldays, only for the challenge of each new paper.

Tea was given to the class in the community parlour the last day. Benedict made a short speech. Five years at the school were over for us, he said. There'd been differences, no one wanted to shut his eyes to the fact, but differences were a fact of life, and they had, if you could put it that way, agreed to differ, and carried on. The important thing was that they had carried on. Now it was over. They were going out from

144

the shade of the school into life . . . it went, and one by one when he had finished we came and thanked him and Brother Patrick.

There was certain pain leaving for the last time, getting the bicycle out of the big room, wheeling over that sanded yard of so much soccer, the lawn and concrete path and lilac tree for the last time, the teachers walking on that concrete in the breaks all the years, up and down, a mystery what they talked about.

Through the green gate with the cross above it facing the Leitrim Road for the last time. Down the town: the shops, Flynn's and Low's, the town clock, past the barracks, and over the stone bridge across the Shannon, Willie Winter's garage and the galvanized paling about the football pitch of the Streets' League.

They were gone, the places in their days, probably able to see them again but never this way, coming from the day of the school. Part of my life had passed in them, it was over, to name them again was to name the dead life as much as them, frozen in the mystery of love.

Yet the surface of it was that I had cycled past them hundreds of evenings without paying the slightest attention. I knew them only now when they were lost, I'd loved them without knowing, and only learned of the love in the losing, and I cycled past the trees and houses of the road, the quarry, afraid to think: and Mahoney read the last paper greedy as he'd read all the others when I got home.

"So it's over," he said. "I'm afraid I wouldn't have made much of a fist of any of it."

"You would if you'd been taught, if you'd studied for it. It wasn't so hard."

"Nothing's hard if you have the know-how, it's only hard if you don't. And you think you managed it alright?"

"I think I did."

"Time'll soon tell that. And whether the others did better."

"That's the question," I was able to laugh. I didn't care, the dice was thrown, I'd have to wait to read its fall, that was all.

"That's the question," Mahoney repeated. "The one certain thing is that there's not places for everyone."

"Dog eat dog," Mahoney muttered in an abstraction over the red paper, the conversation fading.

"Dog eat dog, who'll eat and who'll be eaten, and what'll the eaters and the eaten do," there was at least grim laughter.

"Go on aten, and being et," Mahoney said.

"I suppose."

"May you be lucky anyhow. That's all there's for me to say. And may you be lucky with your luck," he said, an old prayer. He took his hat off the sill. I watched him go.

"There's still work to be done, exams or no exams."

I gathered and put away the books that night. The nights of slavery, cramming the mind for the exam, most of it useless rubbish, and already being forgotten. The most that was left was some of the Latin lyrics, their strange grace; *Macbeth*; some poems; and the delight of solving the maths problems, putting order on their enclosed world, proving that numbers real and imaginary had relationships with each other. That was all. The quicker the rest went out of the head the better. One by one I put the books away, a kind of reverence, my life same as by the shops of the town had passed over these pages, it was over, but there were too many kinds of deaths, and no one's life was very important except to himself or someone else in love with it.

Outside the windows of the room the fields I'd been brought up on stretched to their stone walls, yellow moss and streaks of marvellous white lichen on the grey limestone, some trees green in summer and grazing cattle breaking the green monotony.

24

THE NEXT DAY WAS NEW AND FREE, NO BURDEN OF SCHOOL. HE found old work-clothes and went back with Mahoney to the fields, malleting stakes into the ground to hang barbed wire to split the pastures, and he was painfully soft, arms leaden by the afternoon, barely able to drag feet by night, pissing on the hands and letting the piss dry in an attempt to get the blistering skin hardened. Not able to stay awake after tea, and the night one unconscious sleep till he was woken by clattering buckets late in the yard in the morning, groaning with the ache of the muscles as he put on clothes, out for another day.

Haytime came, the blades of grass shivering on the tractor arm, the turning and the shaking, its dry crackle against the teeth of the raker, the constant rattle of the teeth down again on the hard meadow after lifting free. The fragrance of new hay drenched the evening once the dew started and they were building high the cocks. Joy of a clean field at nightfall as they roofed the last cocks with green grass and tied them down against the wind.

The smell of frying bacon blew from the house as they finished, hay and hayseed tangled in their hair and over their clothes as they walked towards the house, a gentle ache of tiredness. They shared something real at last. They'd striven through the day together, the day was over. No thought or worry anywhere, too tired and at peace to think. The dew was coming down, a white ground mist rising after the heat, a moon pale and quiet above the mushroom shapes of the beeches.

"Twenty cocks in the Big Meadow. Sixteen in the Rock. It'll more than fill the shed. We'll have to throw up a small rick besides. It'll take an Atom Bomb to starve the cattle this winter. No snow will do it," Mahoney laughed his satisfaction into the evening.

"We did a good day," he was content, brown with sun, touched by the extraordinary peace and richness, even the huge docks under the apple trees, of the evening.

There was the delight of power and ease in every muscle now, he'd grown fit and hard, he'd worked into the unawareness of a man's day.

"There's not many would keep pace with the two of us. You've come into your own since the exam."

A hare looped out of the mist and stood. It raised itself, forepaws in the air, one paw crooked, the ears erect. The vague swirl of mist about it seemed to freeze into the intensity of the listening as they stood dead to watch.

It seemed as if it must shudder in the air with the intensity before it fell quietly down again, uncertain, not knowing what way to flee.

"Hulla, hulla, hulla," Mahoney suddenly shouted and it bounded away, disappearing between the green oaks vague at the head of the meadow.

The sleepy cries of the pigeons sounded from Oakport.

"The wood's full of them pigeons. They'll not leave a pick of cabbage on the stumps if they get a chance. They give me the creeps. Cuckoos with hoarse throats."

The tracks of boots left vivid wet splashes on the grass. The frying bacon came stronger, the saliva already too eagerly filling the mouth. Pleasure of drenching the face and arms, the back of the neck, with cold water outside, sitting fresh to the meal on the kitchen table; as later sleep would come before the heaven of a mattress and cool sheets could be enjoyed.

Never was so much work done, fences fixed and egg bushes rooted up, usually left to the winter to do. There was a savage delight in this power and animal strength, the total unconsciousness of the night afterwards. Sundays were spent at football in Charlie's field, the same dogtiredness after, not a shadow of thought. He was a man. He was among men. He was able to take a man's place.

What was strange to notice was that Mahoney was growing old. He'd stop and lean on the pick, panting, "Take it easy. No need to burst yourself. Rome wasn't built in a day."

The cattle got ringworm. They were driven into the cobbled yard, and the wooden gate reinforced with iron bars. Their hooves slid on the cobbles, their eyes great with fear, milling around. For the first time he was their match, he was no longer afraid of a crushing, he had strength enough. He'd coax near, then get an arm around the throats, keep his feet in the first rush till he'd wear them into a corner and grip the sensitive ridge of the nostril between finger and thumb to draw the head up and back, the whites of the eyes rolling, the mouth dripping. He'd hold the heaving flanks of the beast that way against the wall while Mahoney daubed green paint into the sores with a brush.

Mahoney was far the more cautious, a long remove from

149

the days he used shout and bluster on these same cobbles, while the son stood terrified of the charging cattle with the box of green paint and the brush in his hand.

"Watch now. Better men than you got hurt. He'd crack your ribs like a shot against that wall. Maybe we better leave him, and take a chance he'll get alright without the paint, he's too strong," he counselled now.

"No. I think we'll get him. You can put the paint down, and push him into the wall once I catch him. I'll be able to hold him once we get him against the wall."

"But watch, watch, he's as strong as a bull."

The animal was caught and held. Mahoney daubed in the paint. The gate was opened. They all pushed out with the green paint on the sores.

"There's nothing the two of us mightn't do together," Mahoney said as they went, blobs of sweat on his forehead, a weariness in the set of the body, the eyes hunted. He was growing old. Hard to imagine this was the same man who'd made the winters a nightmare over the squalid boots, the beatings and the continual complaining.

They threw away the old raincoats that had protected their clothes, and washed hands and arms in the same basin of hot water with Dettol to kill infection. He watched him there old, and remembered. The looking moved from the cruelty of detachment out into the incomprehension, no one finally knew anything about himself or anybody, even moods of hatred or contempt were passing, were of no necessary consequence.

25

THE EXAM RESULT ARRIVED THE FIRST WEEK IN AUGUST. DAYS
of pestering the postman out on the road ended.

"Anything today?"

The voice shook but tried laughably not to betray its
obvious care, it was an unconcerned question.

"No. Nothing today," he cycled past the gate, amusement
in his voice, mixture of contempt and the superiority of
understanding, the green braid on his tunic.

The day he produced the letter he was forgotten, neither
"Good-bye" nor "Thank you" nor anything. There was no
need to open it to know what it was, the postmark was plain,
Benedict's hand. He just stared at it, the world reduced to its
few square inches. He didn't notice the postman noisily mount
his bike again and cycle off. The problem was how to open it,
it shook violently in his hands. He tore it clumsily at last and

he had to rest it against the gate, his hands were shaking so much, in order to read. His eyes clutched up and down at the words and marks as if to gulp it with the one look into the brain.

It was only slowly it grew clear, the whole body trembling, he'd got the Scholarship, everything. The blue crest of the school crowned the notepaper, Presentation of the Child in the Temple. He started to tremble laughing, tears in the eyes, and then he rested against the gate, it couldn't be true. He read it again.

"I got it. I got it," he burst into the kitchen to Mahoney, hysterically laughing.

"What?"

"The Scholarship, all honours, everything."

Mahoney seized it and read.

"Bejesus, you did it, you did it, strike me pink."

The excitement was changing, he was crying, joy and generosity flowing towards the whole world. He wanted to catch hands and kiss everyone, and dance. He'd buy them presents, bring them places, they were all beautiful. They'd share joy, the world was a beautiful place, all its people beautiful.

"You did it. There's marks for you. That's what'll show them who has the brains round here," Mahoney shouted as he read.

"Congratulations," he shook his hand in the manner of a drama. "Come and congratulate your brother."

They came and shook his hand and smiled up at him with round eyes, and that was the first cooling. They looked at him as different, and he knew he was the same person as before, he'd been given a lucky grace, he wanted it to be theirs as much as his, but he was changed in their eyes, they'd not accept he was the same.

"We'll go to town, the pair of us,' Mahoney was shouting.

"This is no day for work. A day like this won't arrive many times in our lives."

They dressed and went to town. Mahoney talked nonstop on the way, there was nothing to do but be silent and listen. The flood of generosity was choked. He was playing a part in Mahoney's joy, he was celebrating Mahoney's joy and not his own. He grew bored and restless but that was the way the day was going to go.

Let it happen, let it happen, and let it be over as quickly as possible.

"What we'll have to get you first is clothes and shoes. You're someone now. We can't have you looking the part of the ragman."

They went to Curleys, shop of the horror boots for winter.

"Can we help you?" after the shaking of hands.

"We want a whole new outfit for this fellow, he's after getting first place in the University. Scholarship and all Honours in his Leaving. So we can't have him going round like a ragman. Expense is no object. He's going to be someone in the world, not like us."

"Congratulations, it's not every day we have a genius among us."

He went red, such a swamp of embarrassment, he looked round frantic to hide first. Hatred swept against Mahoney: could he not shut his mouth. Three girls in the uniform of black skirt and cardigan were smiling from the women's counter. He thought they were laughing at his cloddish father.

A grey suit was bought, black shoes, a white shirt, and matching wine tie.

"You must be proud today," the manager said to the father. "You deserve great credit for the way you brought these children up."

"We only try to do our best, what more can we do," he diminished but he bloomed in the praise.

153

"There's more than that to it. And now I want to make my own contribution to the happy occasion," and he presented brown leather gloves with the compliments of the house.

"The best shop in the town is Curleys. We got everything we ever wanted here, the best shop in the town."

"We do our best. We value and appreciate our good customers," the manager was pleased too before his staff and came smiling with them to the door.

"The next time it'll be for his father he'll be buying for, we hope, and driving round in a car," Mahoney joked as he backed through the door, so absorbed that he almost flattened a woman passing with parcels. It brought him slightly down to earth, he restored a fallen parcel, and said, "Sorry," to her murderous stare and mutterings.

He was determined on a round of the town, every shop they were known in.

Flynn's where they got *Ireland's Own*.

O'Loan's, the hardware shop.

Even Cassidy's where they got the luxuries of oranges and raisins for Christmas and Easter.

"They have the money but not the brains. This'll be a shake-up for them," he boasted between the shops.

"O'Carroll of Cavan had a son in St. Patrick's and he could be learned nothing. As thick as a solid ditch. So the Reverend President sent for O'Carroll and said, 'You better take away your son, Mr. O'Carroll, we can make nothing of him here,' " he began to recount.

" 'That's alright,' said O'Carroll. 'I'll pay you what you want.'

" 'But he has no brains, Mr. O'Carroll,' the Reverend President said.

" 'Brains, what does he want brains for, I'll buy him brains, the best brains in the country. So keep him.' "

Mahoney laughed loudly at his own story as they paused at

the Public Lavatory in the Shambles, the cobbler's shop in the archway and straw about an abandoned raker in Foley's yard, the cattle pens all around, and lorries from Donegal with bags of cheap potatoes.

"That's one thing can't be bought is brains. Only God can give brains. And they don't come off the wind either."

He made no answer except some phrase of agreement. There was a certain cruelty in the way he watched his father caper but there was the pleasure of attention mixed with the frightful embarrassment of these capers from shop to shop, he was uncomfortable but half-pleased centre of praise.

"The one thing to beware of is a swelled head. That's the ruination of brains. Pride! But if you can keep a cool head you'll show some of them round here how it's done."

26

THE DAY WOULD NOT END PROPERLY WITHOUT THE ROYAL Hotel, its promise of celebration in style. One day they'd dress up and go to town and dine in the Royal Hotel, it was come true at last.

Mahoney ran the comb through his hair, smoothed his lapels, before he pushed through the swing-doors. He demanded the whereabouts of the dining-room from the girl at the cash-desk, trying to cover his unease by aggressiveness. The dining-room was half full, anglers from England for the Arrow trout, commercial travellers, people breaking their journeys. They looked about for a retreat in a corner, or by the river windows, but there were none vacant, and when they did settle for a table they found it was engaged.

"First in first served. There's no fence around it, is there?"

Mahoney attracted the attention of the room by complaining loudly as the waitress led them to another table.

There Mahoney sat at bay, handing the menu card across the table with an assertive flourish.

"Pick what you want. It's your day. It's not every day people get a University Scholarship," he said loud enough for the room to hear, a show of mild interest creeping over the faces, smile of condescending understanding.

Why, why could he not be quiet, why had he to attract attention? What need was there to come here at all, the strain was too shocking, why couldn't they have eaten in a cheap place or gone home? Resentment grew with hot embarrassment. He was beginning to hate the Scholarship. It had been dragged sick through town all day. Now everyone knew here too.

"Whatever you think but shut up about the Scholarship," the first direct protest came.

"You care too much about what people know or think, that's what's wrong with you."

"I don't care and shut up."

"Alright. Alright but there's no need to get so hot. It's your day."

He called the waitress, he was bothered and disturbed, the strange atmosphere, there was no union between them.

"We want the best in the house," he said.

"The chicken is extremely good, sir. Or the duck?" her face remained impassive. He saw on the menu that the duck was the more expensive.

"Duck. Duck for two," he said.

"What will you have with it, sir?" And the rest of the meal was laboriously chosen.

It was not easy to sit through in quiet. Why had the father to try and bulldoze everything through by brute force? The girl was a person too even though she wore the uniform of a waitress. Could he not be quiet just as easy, and ask for what he wanted, the other person had need of dignity too, and he'd get his meal the same in the end.

"You'll have to learn to have more confidence in yourself if you're to be anything in the world. People take you at your own face value. You must stand up for your rights. Never be afraid to go into any place and ask for what you want long as you have money in your pocket. I'm not afraid," he said while she was away.

He didn't answer. This brute assertion made him sick.

"She's a person too," he wanted to say but watched instead the shallow river flowing broken on its stones through the windows, long tresses of green weed swaying in the flow.

The meal was served, embarrassment of not knowing how to use the different knives and forks. They'd been told in school to begin on the outside and work in, but if there happened to be a fault in the arranging, one knife where it shouldn't be, he couldn't think what a country ass he'd seem.

He waited for Mahoney but he plainly didn't know either, watching covertly round at the other tables to see what they were using, joking to cover his unease.

"You'd be able to manufacture a carcass with all this machinery never mind a piece of bloody duck. But this is a meal in style. It must be one of the best hotels this in the West."

Mahoney was in the Royal Hotel, silver and a meal with sauces, he'd have to pay dear, he was determined that he was going to enjoy it. As people left their tables and others came, as the meal wore, he relaxed into a kind of pondering sentimentality.

"We got to the Royal Hotel at last, after all the years. It's a fine meal and a happy day. We've come into our own at last. We're celebrating in style and something to celebrate at last."

"It's a fine meal. Thank you for bringing me."

A vision of how happy the others must be with their tea and bread, free in the house, no burden of what they were not accustomed to.

"No, no thanks at all, it's your day. We've had our differences over the years, there's no house that hasn't, but that's not what counts."

"No. That's not what counts."

"We still love each other after all the years."

"We do."

"We've not been rich but there's love and no hard feelings and that's all that matters. That's what Christ preached."

"Yes. That's all that matters," pressure of Mahoney was driving him crazy, ground underfoot by it, and the walls of the room and people closing round, he'd have to get out of here, if it was only to see the empty street and gulp air on the bridge or watch the river flow out into Key and Rockingham.

"Do you think we could go?"

"It's time I suppose. We'll just get the bill."

He stood. Mahoney was left with no choice. He didn't wait to watch the paying of the bill but waited out in the hall. He felt freer there, but he couldn't be out of the place half quick enough, on the streets with air and people watching or going about their business.

"Do you know what that cost?" Mahoney joined him.

"No."

"Guess."

He guessed deliberately below the price and Mahoney thrust the bill into his hands.

"A disgrace, no wonder they're rotten rich. You pay for the silver and the 'Sir', and the view of the river as if you never saw a river before. Think of all the loaves of bread you could buy for the price of them two meals."

The shops were closing, a grey gentleness entering the light, and the blinds of the pubs were down. People who had no status to uphold were coming out to sit on the bridge. Girls with an air of secrecy about them were going somewhere dressed for the evening. Young men with oil plastering down their hair had come in from the country and stood at the corners with bicycle-clips in their trousers. Girls were sure to pass. Someone might get drunk and make a fool of himself. There might be even a fight or car crash.

"It was a cost but we had to do it. We had to celebrate it. And it's one you'll remember no matter how high you go in the world."

He had to look solemn but he felt free after the hotel and wanted to laugh. He watched his father cycle by his side home, the head low into the wind over the dynamo lamp, pushing. He waited for him to pass the graveyard.

"It gives me the creeps, that place! No matter what happens it winds up there. And you wouldn't mind only there's people dying to get into it," everybody repeated themselves but suddenly at the old joke he wanted to laugh with him and say,

"You are marvellous, my father."

27

IN OCTOBER HE WOULD GO TO THE UNIVERSITY IN GALWAY. THE prospectus was got, £4 sent to Merrion Square in Dublin to buy Matric. The Scholarship was worth £150, thirty weeks in the University year. They allotted it: £40 for fees, £90 for digs, £20 left for books and pocket money, it seemed barely possible.

The whole work changed to the September reaping and binding of the corn with Mahoney, the wild vetch the cattle loved flowered ragged purple in the clean gold, briar and thistle hidden in the rows of fallen oats hurting the hands, but he was hardened by this to these fields between their stone walls.

"What do you think you'll do at the University?" Mahoney probed.

"I'm not sure," he couldn't answer, he couldn't know, it

seemed half unreal that he in old clothes in the cornfield with his father would be at the University before long. The wind swaying through the ripe field, the clashing of the sheaves into stooks, that was all that seemed real.

Benedict came from the school with a photographer, and took his picture before the front wall of the house. They wanted to publish it in the *Herald*.

"You can't hide your light under a bushel these days. It's the age of advertisement," Benedict said.

"He's off to the University and he doesn't even know what he wants to do," Mahoney complained.

"I wouldn't worry about that, he has some idea, I am sure. It's better than to blindly jump at something. It might be no bad idea to go the University, you can spend some time before signing for anything, and look about you."

"There might be some truth in that. More haste less speed I often heard said," Mahoney admitted, and it gave licence to not making a decision. The real days were the days in the field with the rooks black on the pale stooks in the distance, the pigeons clattering from the green oaks.

The photo appeared under *Scholarship Success* with a write-up in which the school's name was prominent underneath. It caused great excitement in the house. Mahoney bought a dozen copies, and posted some away.

"That's what'll shake them up."

He stared more at his own name printed than at the photo. Was that his name, was that him? It was strange to think of people working to print his name and send the newspaper out to the world. Strange to think of all the eyes, in so many different faces, gazing at his name, what would cross their minds as far away as London.

A Monday came for him to go. He said good-bye to the others in the kitchen, hard to smother back emotion, leaving them here, but they didn't see it that way, they were possibly glad not to have to go. The fields through the windows, the stone walls, the trees he knew. It was the hour of the departure at last, the times he'd dreamt about it out of the swamp and suffering of the house, to simply go away, and now that it had come he'd rather remain. The terrified reality of the cleanness of the grain where the red paint had peeled off the gatepost as he went through, the night Mahoney with blobs of sweat on his forehead had first dressed the post in the kitchen, the August day he'd painted it red and protected it a few days later with barbed wire against the cattle. He didn't know what crazy pressures drove him to leave but he left, his overcoat and a suitcase, the other suitcase on the bar of Mahoney's bicycle.

In the October Monday morning they waited for the bus outside Daly's in Bridge Street.

"You know where to go first. Mrs. Ridge of Prospect Hill. Benedict said to give his name and she'd put you up till you found your way about. You have the address?"

"I have."

They stood at the stop. They were joined by others waiting. They made some conversation on the appearances of the others, the appearance and promise of the day, and in the intervals they watched.

"Good-bye. Look after yourself. Write," Mahoney shook hands hurriedly as the bus came in.

"Good-bye. Thanks," he wanted to say it now for everything if he could, no bitterness or anything else in some vision of this parting as both their lives passing utterly alone and lost in time, outside the accidental places and manner of their happening, and then one absolute compulsion to praise or bless.

"Good-bye," the father said again, simply.

"Good-bye," and he was in other people's way, he had to get in. Though he took long putting the cases in the overhead rack the bus didn't go, shaking from the heavy vibration of the running engine. He tried to waste time staring round the bus before he sat down, because all the good-byes were said, but eventually he had to look out. Mahoney was stiff against the wall, staring after someone's shoes, obviously waiting to be released too, and stiffly he walked to the window when he caught his eye. He let the window down, feeling the vibration.

"The bus is due in at twelve-twenty. In less than two hours you'll be there."

"In about two hours."

"You'll not find it go. You'll be able to look out at the country. There are some great fields for mushrooms close to Galway."

"I must watch out. It's lucky it's such a good day."

"Write as soon as you get fixed up."

"I'll write tonight."

The engine revved, it was put in gear, and nosed out from the footpath. The conductor buckled on his ticket machine.

"Good luck," Mahoney waved.

"Good-bye. I'll write tonight."

The bus crossed the bridge. He watched the familiar names on the lintels before it got out of the town, fleeting memories of days he walked between those shops, and then the country road and the fields through the hedges, and he'd said to watch the fields. Close to Galway there were great fields for mush-rooms.

28

"WE DON'T GO IN FOR STUDENTS BUT BECAUSE BROTHER
Benedict sent you we can't see you stuck. You can stay till you
get on your feet and have a chance to look around," Mrs.
Ridge said on Prospect Hill. She was large, heavily handsome,
white hair tinged with blue and worn in a dead fashion,
slowness and assurance in her every movement, the world a
fixed and comfortable place.

She asked much about Benedict as she showed you the
room. "A very clever man and deep, liked everywhere, if
there was more like him in the world it'd be telling," she
praised, brown linoleum under her feet on the stairs and the
shining brass rails, one small yellow rug by the bed; cream
coverlet, wooden wardrobe and table and chair, must be the
same as many rooms, but it was yours, and utterly different.
The corridor was bare and clean, smell of wax and soap, pink

wrappings of Jaffa oranges on a nail beside the seat in the
w.c. When she'd gone you opened your cases, and then gazed
down on the passing street, as it went its imponderable way.

You were given a meal in the restaurant downstairs, a Yale
key, and you went outside, by the green railings of Eyre
Square. You'd a place to stay. You'd money from the Scholarship. You were free. Woolworth's across the Square was the
same as the place in Sligo. A girl with a red scarf walked
ahead, you started to follow, fascination of her shape as she
moved, the cane shopping-basket swinging at her thigh. One
day, one day, one day, you'd have a girl of your own, a world
of marvel then. But now the University, one dream that
would come to earth this day.

You went, asking when you weren't sure, across the Corrib,
two swans against withering October reeds in the distance,
stone buttresses alone in the water, remnants of a railway that
crossed the river to Clifden once. You didn't think. You
were excited. You had the University to see.

Then you saw it through the trees past the boathouse. A
castle, old stone, and towers, green copper domes.

Seat of learning, the gravity of days, eternal evenings,
centre where you'd travel into joys and secrets shut away. The
phrases of rhetoric rose the same as prayers. All the nights of
sweat had meaning now. And why did it cause this rhetorical
reverence or was there anything except the images and these
inconsequential phrases.

But it was hard to walk slow. Wrought iron gates with a
broken gas-lamp on the pier top. The stone lodge and the
chrysanthemums in the beds. A drive of tarmacadam ran past
the front of the main building, rows of old chestnuts bordered
the football pitch and tennis courts, raw colour of a stack of
timber beyond the courts.

It seemed strange to have come, to be standing there on
tarmacadam, and looking on, the images. How much of your

166

life would pass here? You might never even leave. A brilliant course of studies, chosen to teach, a gowned professor under the chestnuts. The roots thick as any tree of the virginia creeper rose to spread and flower red on the stone. The great door with iron bands was open. Notices and letters were tacked on the green boards behind glass. Nobody from your house had ever reached a University before.

Groups stood about. You fell into conversation with a student from Donegal. That night you arranged to go with him to the Savoy. At eight around Moon's Corner he'd meet you.

Afterwards you wandered about the town, you made sure where Moon's Corner and the Savoy was. The bustle of the street seemed to rush as water in a tidal movement, and it was strange to try to understand that you were alive and standing in these busy streets. Outside the Skeffington Arms a boy was crying the evening newspapers. By the Claddagh through the Spanish Arch and out on the Long Walk to the sea, Galway Bay. The *Dun Aongus* was waiting to Aran, a trawler from Rotterdam, the sailors washing its deck with hoses, and the black-headed gulls drifting overhead. Your feet started to tire, you'd walked too much without noticing. The eyes roved, resting for moments on odd objects. Broken fish-boxes and wild grass and the sea, and was it all no more than a catalogue. A sudden flash on the memory, singing of "Galway Bay" under the town clock in Carrick a night after pub close, the drunken voices out of time: and here was where you'd go to the University. You were only hours here yet, and it was not easy to keep hold of the dream, wild grass and sea and broken fish-boxes same as anywhere, this was the University town, but it was more solid concrete and shapes and names with the sea and sky and loneliness than any dream, but at eight you would meet John O'Donnell at Moon's Corner, it was something to look forward to, it would break the obsession that

167

there was never possibility of possession or realization, only the confusion of all these scattered images.

O'Donnell was already waiting when you reached the corner at eight. A shower had started, the streets black and greasy, reflecting the lamps. O'Donnell said he'd looked up the papers, and that there was a terrific cowboy in the Savoy. He'd seen it before in Dublin but wanted to see it again, and immediately you fell into step, it was marvellous to be going with someone to any picture. You got the cheapest seats, close to the screen, each of you paying for his own. A short, "Jingle Tunes" was running when you entered the dark, people were singing, and O'Donnell was hardly in his seat when he joined them.

> On top of Old Smokey
> All covered with snow, (everyone together)
> I lost my true lover
> Came a courtin' too slow.

O'Donnell was singing, without any self-consciousness in the world. You couldn't. People were all about. You wished you could join too but it was no use, would it be same as this always, but it was still wonderful to be just there. This was life.

"Come on. Sing up. We used go crazy over this in the Royal in Dublin with Tommy Dando."

"I can't. I'm not used."

And then with relief the cowboy was running, there was silence, the cinema was lost in what was happening on the one screen. There was a feeling of being set free to share in all this running and excitement, the strong righteous man and the noble woman against the hirelings. Out on the wet street afterwards there were several heroes with gun hand crooked and unflinching walk ready to shoot their way through to the world.

"What did you think?" O'Donnell asked.

"It was great," you managed to say out of the choking after effect of the emotion, all pictures were marvellous, you hadn't seen enough to compare, people who said one was good and another bad had some secret knowledge.

"It was smashing. Do you want to head home or would you like a cup of coffee?"

"I don't mind, whatever you'd like."

"We'll have a cup."

You paid when the waitress brought the cups, everything was plastic, the cups and spoons to the green table-top.

"Used you go to the pictures much?" you asked once the cups were stirred.

"In Dublin, always on Sunday afternoon, and other times if there was a girl and any money. That's when we were in the Albert College."

"Where used you get the girls?" you were fearful of betraying your ignorance, the trembling curiosity.

"At the dances. Every Sunday night we were in Conarchy's. Always more women than men. They say Dublin is the best place in the world for women."

"What kind were the women?"

"Fine things. Nurses, and girls from Cathal Brugha. They used to live in a hostel in Mountjoy Square. Schweppes Lane was a great place beside the hostel, full of couples after Conarchy's."

Over the coffee-cups a pain of jealousy. Schweppes Lane crowded with couples, kissing and touching in the lane's darkness, where did they put hands, or did they strip clothes against the wall. O'Donnell had been there against the soft flesh of a girl out of Conarchy's, and you hadn't, that much pleasure escaped from your life for ever.

"Have you any girl?" O'Donnell asked.

"No. I can't dance," you said, though for a moment you were tempted to lie.

"No one can dance. They just shuffle round. It's a place to pick up girls. If you watch for a dance or two you get the hang of it. Why not come to the Jib's Dance Thursday night? After that we could hit out to Seapoint."

The Jib's Dance was in the Aula Maxima. The coloured poster in the archway had displayed a cloddish couple dancing.

"Do you think would I be able?"

"Of course," O'Donnell laughed.

The café was closing. At Moon's Corner you parted. O'Donnell had to cross the river past the University. It was still raining. Eyre Square was lit more with neon than the lamps. You began to touch the wet iron railings with your fingers for no reason as you walked, listened to your feet go on the pavement. You wished you could have walked with O'Donnell, even though you'd have to come back across the sleeping town on your own, and you wished you could find someone to talk any rubbish with when you reached Prospect Hill, anything to avoid the four walls of the room and the electric light on the bed, but it was too late, you had to climb on the stairs creaking under your feet on the bare brown linoleum. When you switched on the light you shivered to see the cream coverlet flood bare with light. You had come to the University, you'd sleep your first night in the town. You thought of Mahoney in another bed in the same night, and that you'd promised to write, it'd pass some of the time, it'd be something to do now.

You wrote to a formula on the glass-covered dressing-table. You'd arrived safely, you'd got digs, you'd seen the town and the University, tomorrow you'd be enrolled. You hoped they were well and that they'd write soon.

You left the letter ready for posting in the morning, and then undressed with a sort of melancholy deliberation. You'd come at last to the University and you'd still to take off your clothes, drape them on the back of the chair. It was the death of the day, and the same habitual actions of the funeral as always, and no matter what happened all days and lives ended this way. Only longing and dream changed.

As you pulled back the corner of the sheets you knelt, mechanically going through the night prayers, what you'd not done for months, sense of the shocking space and silence of the world about your own perishing life in the room lessened by the habitual words and the old smell of camphor from the sheets in which your face was buried.

In the double bed you lay awake for long, listening to cars close and fade, and the fascination of feet you knew nothing about go by on the concrete underneath the window.

29

THE DREAM WAS TORN PIECEMEAL FROM THE UNIVERSITY before the week was over. Everyone wanted as much security and money as they could get.

"What are you doing?" was the conversation under the notices in the archway.

"Dentistry."

Why?

"It's about the best. There's a shortage. You can earn £4,000 a year. The initial cost of the equipment to start out with is the worst, but there's a lot of hard cash in it after that."

Will teeth absorb your life?

"No, but you can get interested in anything if you're at it long enough and if you've enough money it can compensate for a lot. If you have to be scraping all the time for money see how long you'll be happy."

And money was dream enough to soldier on too. Choice of

car and golf club and suburban house, grade A hotels by any sea in summer, brandy and well-dressed flesh.

"Security. Security. Everyone's after security. And the only gilt-edged security to be had is the kingdom of heaven," the Reverend Bull Reegan thumping at the old annual retreats in Carrick.

The college had opened. You'd listened to the President's address, a white-haired Monsignor, saying something about an idea of a university in Gaelic, with many quotations—and no one able to follow.

Classes had commenced, and still you didn't know what to do. You drifted from one lecture to another, soon you'd have to decide.

"The Association of Scientists estimates that by 1968 the present serious shortage of scientists will have more than doubled. But standards are rising. Last year out of a class of thirty-two no more than fourteen passed their B.Sc. You must have aptitude and be prepared to work. It is no place for the frivolous. But those who qualify can be assured of a well remunerated position."

The appearance of the lecturer didn't seem to matter as you left, neither his shape nor features nor the clothes he wore, he was what he said. The University was here. Green oaks lined the boundary wall. Farther out was Galway Bay. Everybody in the world was supposed to be unique.

"Unless you have private incomes the majority of you doing English must know that you'll wind up teachers if you're lucky, which has its compensations, though affluence is unlikely to be numbered among them. If there are any among you who have literary ambitions the evidence would seem to point to a dosshouse or a jail as a more likely place of genesis than a University," and went on to say that nothing interfered so much with his day as the unaesthetic sight of students lounging on the drive when he came in and out.

On the walk as he was laughed at afterwards, you'd heard them say that he had only one real ambition, to drive to Dublin in under three hours, he'd already had several crashes in the attempt.

Though there were one or two who simply spoke about their subject with love, and their quiet excitement was able to come through, one frail grey-haired woman in a botany class, a younger man at mathematics who continually brushed imaginary chalk specks from his gown as he spoke and you came away wanting to learn and share, both were beautiful and young in some way.

Your doubts grew as you wandered, you wanted less and less to stay the more you saw, but it was easier to stay than go. It was clear that there'd be little dream, mostly the toil of lectures, and at night the same swotting and cramming in a room for the exams same as last year. You wondered as you came home by Eglington Street at four if it'd be long till the E.S.B. clerkships were announced, they were based on the Leaving results, you'd entered the same as the others, and the same marks that got the Scholarships were bound to get high there too. If you stayed you'd have to choose some course before the end of this week, this dithering had a limit, you thought it had to be Science. The fees were too high for medicine. Six years was too long a course. Science was three years. A job was certain at its end. Fear close to despair came at the image of failing or getting sick or losing the Scholarship, you'd have to fall back on Mahoney for support. It was frightening.

The night was the night of the Jibs' Dance in the Aula, a new poster was up in the archway, you'd to meet John O'Donnell inside at nine.

The preparations took over an hour, shaving and washing, clean white shirt and collar out of the case, shining of the shoes, brushing of every speck from the suit, the hair flattened with Brylcream, the teeth brushed, the painful knotting and unknotting of the wine tie before the mirror, diarrhoea of tension.

What would it be like, the band, the music, the dances, the women? Would you be scorned by these women?

Because you couldn't dance.

Were you good-looking enough, would they look at you with revulsion?

Would you by watching pick up the steps and rhythms of the dance?

Would you have courage to ask a girl to dance?

Would you find yourself on the floor trampling on her feet, not able to dance, saying, "I'm sorry. I'm not able to dance, I'm only learning," and would she leave you in the middle, "You'd better pick someone else to learn on," or would she endure you in stony silence?

What would you talk to a girl about?

Would you be able to endure the white softness of her bare arm, the rustle of taffeta or the scent of lacquer when she leaned her hair close, without losing control and trying to crush her body to yours?

Would you be the one leper in the hall at Ladies Choice, flinching as every woman in the place casually inspected and rejected you, their favour falling on who was beside you, the other men melting like snow about you until you stood a rejected laughing stock out on the floor in the way of the dancers, no woman would be seen with you? It would be as if your life was torn out of your breast by every couple dancing together and you could slink towards the shadow of the pillars, fit to weep, watch your own mangled life go dancing past.

"Off to the dance," they said downstairs as you went.

"Off to the dance," you repeated and pressed your features into an embarrassed smile.

175

"All the girls will be falling for him tonight, but don't do anything we wouldn't do."

"No. Good night."

Laughter wreathed about their "Good night", and was it mockery.

Down the hill to Eyre Square and coldness of the night on your flushed face and by Moon's Corner down Eglington Street. It was after nine on the clocks, every step brought you nearer to your first dance and you wished they went in the opposite direction. It would be so easier to hang about the streets, but you'd promised to meet John O'Donnell beside the bandstand at nine, it was already past nine. With a sinking of the guts you crossed the Weir Bridge round the canal, the high jail wall there, and the footpath under the green oaks up University Road. There were all lights about the college, and it was surely music you could hear. Your feet slowed, you let your eyes close, if only you could turn back.

Inside the lodge gates there was some commotion. You crossed the other side of the road, glad of any excuse of delay, the blood pounding at the temples, you felt you could sit all night on a lavatory bowl. The hands were trembling.

"Control yourself. Control yourself. It's not the end of the world. It'll be forgotten by tomorrow morning," but it was no use.

"You can't face it," the nerves shivered.

"If you don't go to this dance it'll be even harder the next time, you'll never be able to go, you'll never be able to take any natural part in life, get any natural fulfilment. You'll be an oddity all your days.

"No. No. I'm not able to face it. I'm sick. Another night it'll be easier."

You'd drawn a most level with the gates on the opposite pavement. If you stood and stopped the crazy fighting within yourself you'd be able to see what the noise inside the gates was. It was a crowd of students out of range of the lodge lamp under the chestnuts. A pair of girls with college scarves passed in. The shouting started up again into a foxtrot drifting from within the quadrangle. The words were easy enough to catch out of the general howl as the girls came level.

> You're out for your onions tonight.
> Bless me, mother, for I'm going to sin.
> Get them off you. Get them off you.
> Dance, mother, dance.

The phases could be picked out before the shouting rose to one general howl of derision as the girls hurried up the drive to the main door.

A single man student went through the gates, the same performance started under the trees. He paid no attention. He continued along the drive, in the one unruffled stride, and that was the way to go past, but you were certain by this that you wouldn't go past, perhaps you'd not pass even if they weren't there, they were no more than the easy way out you'd be looking for all along. You stood on the pavement and watched and listened. The music came over the short distance from the quadrangle, changed to a quickstep you recognized from some sponsored radio programme.

A vision of the dance floor came to plague you, naked shoulders of the women, glitter of jewellery on their throats, scent and mascara and the blood on their lips, the hiss of silk or taffeta stretching across their thrusting thighs, and always their unattainable crowned heads floated past. And you stood on the pavement outside the lodge gates.

This was the dream you'd left the stern and certain road of the priesthood to follow after, that road so attractive now since you hadn't to face walking it any more, and this world of sensuality from which you were ready to lose your soul not so easy to drag to your mouth either for that one destructive kiss,

177

as hard to lose your soul as save it. Only in the mind was it clear.

You turned away, back towards the town, not able to return to the room because of the shame if you were seen slink through the hallway, you'd have to wait till they were sleeping or the dance was over.

You walked, it soothed and gathered back calm in some way, along the rotting network of the canals, stars caught between the invading grass and reeds, the flour-mills at the bridges and not many about under the lamps, your life and all life a strange thing.

In the café, over cups of coffee, in Shop Street, you spent the last part of the night; here you'd sat with John O'Donnell after the Savoy; and tonight he was dancing.

You envied the old waitress, she seemed asleep in everything she did, there were worse lives. All day she served nondescript customers that came through the swing doors, tired on her feet at the end, the one desire to get back to her bed and room, but perhaps it wasn't as simple as that either, perhaps nothing was. When the café was closing, chairs being stacked on some of the tables, you made your way back to Prospect Hill. It was after twelve, and the dance should have been about over. By this time it didn't seem to matter whether anyone was up or not to ask you about the dance. You felt like telling them the truth, and as violently as possible, it'd be some compensation.

The next morning two letters were waiting when you came down; one from Mahoney, the other had been redirected, it was typed, with a Dublin postmark. When you tore it open it was from the E.S.B. You were asked to present yourself for a medical examination in Dublin on Monday, and if passed, you should be ready to take up employment with the Board almost immediately.

It'd be pleasant to walk to work on a fine morning through

178

the streets of Dublin, to have pay coming at the end of each week, to be free for ever from dependence on Mahoney, to be able to go to Croke Park Sunday afternoons, and to be free. Chained to a desk all day would be the worst part, but there was money for it, and freedom. Staying here at the University would be three years of cramming rubbish into the mind in constant dread of sickness and failure at the exams. You just couldn't go home defeated to Mahoney.

It was strange this morning leaving Prospect Hill in the rain, through Eyre Square for the last time or the beginning of every morning for the next three years, you'd have to answer the letter this evening, dallying was over, you'd have to answer it one way or the other. You'd have to choose.

With a new detachment you watched the goalposts, strangely luminous in the rain, the green onion domes, and the first classes of the day. You'd have to make up your mind to stay here or leave before this evening, and then an absurd accident struck that removed all detachment.

The Physics Theatre was full, the seats rising in stairs to the back, and the waiting crowd shouting and beginning to grow restless when a white-coated attendant entered with some apparatus for an experiment. The restlessness became directed at the little attendant. He was loudly cheered down to the table, feet were stamped, the theatre close to a football match when the lecturer red with fury appeared.

In a second dead silence fell.

"I won't tolerate hooliganism in my class now or at any other time," the lecturer, small with glasses, thundered, and there wasn't even a stirring of feet.

It was strange, the sudden deadly silence in place of the shouting, and his fury too big in some way for the small man with the glasses, several of the students who were dumb now could have taken him in their hands and thrown him out the window.

"I'll tolerate no hooliganism in my class," the small lecturer who would teach physics through Irish and who'd told them in the previous class that he'd found no difficulty in following lectures in Germany once he'd got over the initial newness of the language, and he saw no reason why they shouldn't be able to do the same through Irish, shouted again from the table, and it suddenly seemed too comic, the huge *hooliganism* too big in his mouth, and the students roaring a minute ago, quiet as mice before him, and you made the mistake of smiling.

"Get out you," he pointed.

Whoever was next you stood.

"No. Not you. The gentleman on your left."

It couldn't be, you were suddenly bewildered, but stood expecting it to be someone else.

"What's your name?"

The room swam, you were hardly able to answer, there was sense of bewildering unreality, everyone must be looking at you. You'd been quiet, but why had you to cursed smile.

"Get out. I won't take hooliganism in my class now or at any other time."

Awkwardly you got out of the bench, the others standing to make way, and you were alone on the wooden steps of the passage without strength to climb, sense of that mass to your left staring at you, and the shock and shame. You wanted to weep when you'd got through the door, it had happened too quick to comprehend, the shock was too sudden, and you stood dazed on the quadrangle in the rain.

"The pompous little fucker and *hooliganism* filling his mouth," but why had this cursed shame and misfortune to fall on you before any of the others. On the wet tarmacadam you went at snail's pace towards the archway, trying to go over what had happened, and the crippling flush of shame when you did, over and over as you went on towards the archway.

"Is there something wrong?" an older student approached in the archway.

"He threw me out of the Physics class," it was relief to tell.

"Was it Brady?"

"Yes."

"He always does that at the beginning of every year, what did he fire you for?"

"There was a racket when he came in and I smiled or something after the rest were stopped. I hadn't been doing a thing before," you were hardly able to get it out, but you had fierce need.

"Did he ask your name?"

"He did. Does that make any difference?"

"You'll have to apologize to him and ask him to allow you back."

"And is it serious?"

"Brady always fires someone at the start of the year."

"Does he let them back?"

"He does. The only thing you'd want to watch is that he doesn't fire you again. If he happened to get his knife in you, you might as well clear out."

"When could you apologize?"

"Before or after some class. If I were you I'd leave it till tomorrow though. He'll let you back all right. He proves himself like this every year."

You went down the tarmacadam, Brady's cursed class in progress to your right, out under the drips of the green oaks along University Road. The tar shone in the rain. The town faced you, smoke mixed in the rain above the houses. You'd to make up your mind. Either to go and apologize to Brady and face three years cramming here or go to Dublin to the job. It wasn't Brady drove you, you'd go and crawl for him if it was worth it, only a fool stood up, you could go and crawl and savage him after if you got the chance and wanted still.

But maybe it was the fall of the dice, you were meant to go, and if anything happened here there was no one to turn to, not Mahoney. It was better to go and it'd be better to do it at once and tell Mahoney.

In the post office near Moon's Corner you wasted several telegram forms till you were finally satisfied with,

WANT TO TAKE E.S.B. AND LEAVE UNI., WILL WAIT FOR
YOUR CONSENT

They said at the counter that he'd have it in about two hours.

30

MAHONEY CAME THE NEXT MORNING, FULL OF A SENSE OF drama. There was an important decision to be made. He'd play in it to the last.

"You want to leave?"

"I do."

"Well, we'll have to think about it, a rash decision now could cause your whole life to regret it. We'll have to discuss it, get advice about it, only fools rush rashly."

The suitcase was in your father's hand, it was weird or strange walking with him in Eyre Square, this older man might as well not be father at all, and children were chanting *Eena meena-mina-mo, Catch a nigger by the toe,* outside the green railings.

"I thought you wanted to be a doctor?"

"No. The course is too long. The Scholarship only lasts

four years, the fees are too high. It'd be impossible on the Scholarship."

"That's to be considered alright," a lot of the swagger disappeared, it was no longer a play, it might involve forking out money.

"With the E.S.B., I'd be earning money straight away," you'd learned long ago the kind of reasons to present, no use giving your own reasons, but reasons closest to where it touched Mahoney.

"We'll have to take everything into consideration. After I got the telegram I dressed up and went in to see Brother Benedict. He said that under no circumstances should I allow you leave. He said you had a brilliant career in front of you at the University, and that you'd rot in an office. That's one opinion. What we'll have to do is thrash the whole thing out, and come to the best decision, so that there be no regrets after."

He was impatient of any interruption, he gesticulated violently as well as raising his voice to drown the one attempt you made to say that you'd already decided. You'd take the E.S.B. and it'd be your own decision.

"But what we'll have to get first is something to eat. An empty bag can't stand never mind think. After we see to the inner man we'll see what way the road lies."

Over the meal in the restaurant he aired it.

"This lad of mine wants to leave the University and go to the E.S.B. It has me worried. It's hard to know what way to advise."

"A steady job has a lot to be said for it. He might waste years at the University and not do as good at the heel of the hunt. Drinking and dancing is what some of them I see are best qualified for on leaving here," a little man in a tweed suit, spectacles on his nose, who was in the Good's Store of the railway station, voiced.

"The E.S.B. is the same as a government job, it can't go down. He'd have a pay straight away, an increment every year, his chances for promotion, and a pension. In no time he'd be able to settle down and have his own little home," was Mrs. Ridge's contribution.

"I don't agree with that, he's young, he's plenty of time to worry about security. At his age he should take a chance. It's the only interesting thing to do," a young policeman, who was obviously dissatisfied with his own position, contradicted.

"It'll be his own decision anyway. I'll not interfere. He won't have me to blame in after years. That's the only sure thing," Mahoney bloomed in the attention.

You watched Mahoney with cold and hidden fury, you'd been in this restaurant days and they'd learned more about you in this half-hour than all the days together. All this air of importance and wisdom breathed through their cigarette smoke was horrible, it was your life they talked about, but soon it'd be over.

"I'll not be going home till tomorrow and I was wondering if you'd be able to fix me up for the night," Mahoney asked after the meal.

"We'll fix you up, but you won't have a room. It's either fix a bed for you downstairs or the double bed is big enough for two since it'll be only for one night. That's if you don't mind," Mrs. Ridge said.

"Not at all. We're easy. That has the whole thing solved. Thanks very much. You're very good, Mrs. Ridge."

"That's great. Everything is settled for the night, you feel easier, and do you know I was thinking that the best thing we could do is get a priest's advice. The Franciscans of Galway are famous, they're gentle the Franciscans, more like ordinary people," Mahoney said soon as they were alone on the streets.

"What good would that do?"

"A priest is sort of on the fence. They can see better. We

185

could go and put your case and I am sure we wouldn't get bad advice."

"Alright so," it would finish it, moments it seemed once talk had started that it might be better to take the risk and stay at the University. Chained to a desk in Dublin no matter what security attended it might prove no easier bed of roses, all this deciding was a horror.

"I think if we're to get advice, one of the Deans of Residence at the College would be best. That's his job, to look after students, he'd know more about that kind of problem than the Franciscans."

"That's alright so, as long as it's some priest," Mahoney agreed.

You walked across the town, father and son, and when you met students from the University you were ashamed of your father, and then fiercely loathed yourself for being ashamed, there was no real reason, except stupid resentment of your own unique identity being associated with your father, you'd be linked with and associated with your father, instead of being utterly alone and free against a background of snow.

"So this is the University," Mahoney wondered. "A bit on the style of a castle. It'd cost a quare penny to put up a building like that nowadays, even if they had the tradesmen."

It was the University, you looked at it, the shambles of a dream. Never would you walk again with a dream through the archway and by the canal through the Spanish Arch and out towards the sea on the Long Walk. You'd swot towards the B.Sc. here or you'd leave it for the E.S.B.

The Dean received you in his office without any waiting: the Dean, a tall lean man with eyes that weren't easy to meet, they were cold and sharp.

"I am a student here. I have a Scholarship. I have been offered a clerkship in the E.S.B. My father thought you might

186

be able to advise us what to do," you tried to put it bare as possible, awkward and a fool in the stumbling words.

"That's right, father," it was relief that Mahoney was staying in the background.

"Which would you like to do yourself?" the priest probed calmly.

"I don't know, father."

"What course did you intend to follow?"

"Science I think, father."

"You don't have any keen interest in it?"

"No, father. It'd be easy to get a job out of it afterwards. I wanted to do Medicine first, but the course is too long. The Scholarship is only for four years."

"What do you feel about staying on at the University?"

"I don't know, father. It's not like I thought it'd be," you saw both of you look mean and shabby in the priest's eyes.

"If you're a scholarship boy, you'll probably do well at the University. If you did you'd get a much more pleasant job than the E.S.B. out of the University. So I think you should stay," what he said was like shock of cold water, he was too clever to give advice, he was throwing down the gauntlet to see if you had the wish to pick it up and he knew you hadn't. And you saw and resented his calculated probing or attack.

"I'm afraid I might get sick or fail and there's more in the house besides me, father," and it sounded as lame as it was.

"You're afraid of failing?"

"I am, father."

"You'd not have to worry about that in the E.S.B.," the priest looked you straight in the face and you saw what he was doing and hated him for it. The Dean was forcing you to decide for yourself.

"No. I'd not have to worry."

"Well, I definitely think you should take the E.S.B. so," there seemed contempt in his voice, you and Mahoney would never give commands but be always menials to the race he'd come from and still belonged to, you'd make a schoolteacher at best. You might have your uses but you were both his stableboys, and would never eat at his table.

It was hard to walk quiet out of the University at Mahoney's side and see the goalposts luminous in the grey light of the rain and not give savage expression to one murderous feeling of defeat.

Though not even that lasted for long, the rage and futility gradually subsiding as you walked through the streets of that wet day. What right had anybody or anything to defeat you and what right had you to feel defeated, who was to define its name?

One day, one day, you'd come perhaps to more real authority than all this, an authority that had need of neither vast buildings nor professorial chairs nor robes nor solemn organ tones, an authority that was simply a state of mind, a calmness even in the face of the turmoil of your own passing.

You could go to the E.S.B. If it was no use you could leave again, and it didn't matter, you could begin again and again all your life, nobody's life was more than a direction.

You were walking through the rain of Galway with your father and you could laugh purely, without bitterness, for the first time, and it was a kind of happiness, at its heart the terror of an unclear recognition of the reality that set you free, touching you with as much foreboding as the sodden leaves falling in this day, or any cliche.

31

In the bedroom that night on Prospect Hill the rosary
was said before undressing. There was morbid fascination in
watching Mahoney take off his clothes, down to the long
johns, some obscenity about the yellow shade of the wool, and
the way they stretched below the knees, the curly hair of the
leg between that and the ankle.

Memories of the nightmare nights in the bed with the
broken brass bells came, and it was strange how the years had
passed, how the nights were once, and different now, how this
night'd probably be the last night of lying together.

"That's a relief," he sighed as he sank down into a creak of
springs. "The town wears you out. You walk miles without
noticing, each street is so short."

"Not being used to the concrete probably accounts for it
too."

"Well, we decided anyhow. So let's hope for the best. It's a relief to me too. The University had me worried. I'd never have told you though only you've decided this way. I wasn't going to interfere with your decision. It had to be your own. But I'm the father to the others as well. I have to think about them as well. I was worried."

"It's the best decision I think."

"You'll go to Dublin tomorrow?"

"At nine. They said at the station that the early train goes at nine. The early train would give more chance to look around."

"Are you sure you don't want me to go with you?"

"I'm certain. The whole thing's caused you enough trouble already. And there's no need. I'll be able to manage."

"It'd be no trouble to go if I could be of any use."

"No. There's no need. I'll get a place."

"If you're stuck ask a policeman. You can take the number on his tunic if you feel there's anything fishy about him."

"I can do that if I'm stuck. Any place that looks alright will do till I get my feet. I can look around then."

"Take a good look at the place first. Dublin's not like down here."

"I'll do that. Will you go back tomorrow?"

"I will. On the bus. All you do in a place like this is waste money."

There was the muffled sounds of movement in another bedroom, the stirring silence of a house at night. Feet continually passed on the concrete underneath the window.

"You're going out into the world on your own now?"

"I am."

"We won't be together any more. There was good times and bad between us, as near everywhere, but it's not what counts much."

"No. It's not what counts."

"We were often cooped up too much in that house but we came through in spite of everything. That's what is important. And you thrashed them all, and got the Scholarship. That was one good day we had, the day we went to the Royal Hotel."

"It was a good day. I enjoyed that day very much. It cost you a lot of money."

"A splash like that now and again is no harm. Going on all the time in the same way would land you soon in the mad-house."

"That's right. I never thought of it that way."

"Things happened in all that time, none of us are saints. Tempers were lost. You don't hold any of that against me, I don't hold anything against you."

"No. I wouldn't have been brought up any other way or by any other father."

"It might have been better if your mother had to live. A father doesn't know much in a house. But you know that no matter what happened your father loves you. And that no matter what happens in the future he'll love you still."

"And I'll always love you too. You know that."

"I do."

It seemed that the whole world must turn over in the night and howl in its boredom, for the father and for the son and for the whole shoot, but it did not.

Beyond the constant passing of feet on the concrete underneath the window a train shunted.

"We better try and go to sleep."

"We'd be better. We have to be early afoot in the morning."

"Good night so, Daddy."

"Good night, my son. God bless you."

FOR THE BEST IN PAPERBACKS, LOOK FOR THE 🐧

In every corner of the world, on every subject under the sun, Penguin represents quality and variety—the very best in publishing today.

For complete information about books available from Penguin—including Puffins, Penguin Classics, and Compass—and how to order them, write to us at the appropriate address below. Please note that for copyright reasons the selection of books varies from country to country.

In the United Kingdom: Please write to *Dept. EP, Penguin Books Ltd, Bath Road, Harmondsworth, West Drayton, Middlesex UB7 0DA.*

In the United States: Please write to *Penguin Putnam Inc., P.O. Box 12289 Dept. B, Newark, New Jersey 07101-5289* or call 1-800-788-6262.

In Canada: Please write to *Penguin Books Canada Ltd, 10 Alcorn Avenue, Suite 300, Toronto, Ontario M4V 3B2.*

In Australia: Please write to *Penguin Books Australia Ltd, P.O. Box 257, Ringwood, Victoria 3134.*

In New Zealand: Please write to *Penguin Books (NZ) Ltd, Private Bag 102902, North Shore Mail Centre, Auckland 10.*

In India: Please write to *Penguin Books India Pvt Ltd, 11 Panchsheel Shopping Centre, Panchsheel Park, New Delhi 110 017.*

In the Netherlands: Please write to *Penguin Books Netherlands bv, Postbus 3507, NL-1001 AH Amsterdam.*

In Germany: Please write to *Penguin Books Deutschland GmbH, Metzlerstrasse 26, 60594 Frankfurt am Main.*

In Spain: Please write to *Penguin Books S. A., Bravo Murillo 19, 1° B, 28015 Madrid.*

In Italy: Please write to *Penguin Italia s.r.l., Via Benedetto Croce 2, 20094 Corsico, Milano.*

In France: Please write to *Penguin France, Le Carré Wilson, 62 rue Benjamin Baillaud, 31500 Toulouse.*

In Japan: Please write to *Penguin Books Japan Ltd, Kaneko Building, 2-3-25 Koraku, Bunkyo-Ku, Tokyo 112.*

In South Africa: Please write to *Penguin Books South Africa (Pty) Ltd, Private Bag X14, Parkview, 2122 Johannesburg.*